Chapter One

It squatted on the tarmac like a bloated dragonfly, a little bigger and a lot older than she'd expected. Painted a drab green with half a dozen random splashes of other colors, it had obviously been in service for decades.

Chelsea had never flown in a helicopter before. She would have thought the stress of the past few weeks might have left her too worn-out for nerves, but nope, turned out that wasn't the case. She held the bouquet of roses closer to her body and approached a man she took to be the pilot, who, wrench in hand, was peering into the open engine compartment. Was that a bad omen?

He looked up at the sound of her footsteps and broke into a welcoming grin. "You must be Ms. Pierce," he said as he closed the cover and secured it.

"Chelsea, please. And you're Mr. Black?"

"Heck, call me Bobby. Everyone does except my ex-wife and you don't want to know the words she uses." He tucked the wrench into his pocket, stuck out his hand, apparently noticed all the grease smudges and plucked a rag from his belt instead. Tall and rangy with a touch of gray in his hair, it was impossible not to hear the lingering drawl of Texas in his voice. Chelsea opened her purse and withdrew the requested money order, made out for the amount he'd specified. It was a lot of money for her, and now, as she peered over his shoulder at the aging chopper, she second-guessed her decision to hire him.

Really, would that thing fly? Was it safe?

He apparently sensed her hesitation. "Don't underestimate old Gertie," he said, patting the drab metal. "She's been around, sure—heck, so have I—but we're both fit as a fiddle. I have our route mapped out. I'll get close enough to drop those roses." His gaze darted from the flowers to the money order.

For a second, she contemplated walking away but her peace of mind was at stake and that was no small matter.

Chelsea had found this guy on the internet—he was the only one she could afford—and had spoken to him on the phone. She'd outlined her plan and been assured it was a piece of easy-peasy pie. Then she'd asked her sister, Lindy, to run the food truck for a few days and driven from San Francisco toward Nevada, spent the night in a motel where the cockroaches were bigger than her shoes, counted out fifty dollars for flowers and allowed her heart to embrace the possibility of closure.

And now she was going to give up because the helicopter looked a little…tired?

Steven's face floated through her mind. Gray eyes that ranged in shade from hazy morning dawn to early evening twilight, lips that caused her heart to flutter, a killer body topped off by a soul as deep as the sea.

"You saved my life."

He touched her face. To his relief, she didn't sweep his hand away and instead covered his fingers with hers. "Don't cry," he said softly. "It's going to be okay. I promise I won't let anything happen to you. Now, get some sleep, okay?"

"Maybe tomorrow I'll wake up with all my memories intact," she whispered.

"I hope so," he said, and once again fought the urge to kiss her. By the time he'd zipped the flap closed again, she'd rolled onto her side, and he switched off the lantern.

He used the flashlight to make a bed on the ground, curled into the sleeping bag and closed his eyes. If she was determined to leave him, he'd have to let her go, but somehow he'd have to come up with a way to prepare her for the return of her memories. How would Chelsea handle the moment when she realized that Adam was her beloved Steven, and that instead of dead and gone, he was very much alive and on the run?

HIDDEN IDENTITY

ALICE SHARPE

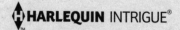

This book is dedicated, with love,
to Annabelle Marie Zi-Ling Yu.

ISBN-13: 978-1-335-60425-5

Hidden Identity

Recycling programs
for this product may
not exist in your area.

Copyright © 2019 by Alice Sharpe

Printed in U.S.A.

www.Harlequin.com

Alice Sharpe met her husband-to-be on a cold, foggy beach in Northern California. Their union has survived the rearing of two children, a handful of earthquakes, numerous cats and a few special dogs, the latest of which is a yellow Lab named Annie Rose. Alice and her husband now live in a small rural town in Oregon, where she devotes the majority of her time to pursuing her second love, writing. You can write to her c/o Harlequin Books, 195 Broadway, 24th Floor, New York, NY 10007. An SASE for reply is appreciated.

Visit the Author Profile page at Harlequin.com.

CAST OF CHARACTERS

Adam Parish—When the witness protection plan fails him, Adam's forced to implement a drastic plan of escape. He knows leaving his fiancée behind will break her heart, but at least she'll be safe—or so he thinks. Too late, he finds out she makes perfect bait. Now it's up to him to keep her and her precious cargo alive.

Chelsea Pierce—Grief-stricken, she seeks to put the past behind her. She's close to accomplishing this when her world comes crashing down. Will she recover in time to realize that fate has handed her a second, dazzling chance?

Devin Holton—It appears even a prison cell can't contain this man's lust for revenge or his ability to hire as many killers as it takes to accomplish his goal.

Whip Haskins—Adam's longtime mentor and friend sworn to help Adam stay alive.

Ron Ballard—This US marshal has the connections to carry out elaborate assassin schemes. Is he on Holton's payroll?

Aimee Holton—What is Devin Holton's selfish wife up to and what will she and her minions do to protect themselves?

Tom Nolan—Aimee's new lover and partner. How deep does his collusion go?

With him, she'd embraced the concept of forever. And now he was gone.

How did a relationship that lasted only a few weeks produce such profound fallout including so many unanswered questions? Police found evidence of a struggle and gunshots in his empty house but no victims. She'd been frantic at first, then informed by various "officials" that Steven had driven to a small out-of-town airport, retrieved his plane and flown away.

Flown away? He had a plane? Where did he go? And why didn't he take her with him?

One of the officials, a fifty-year-old guy named Ballard, managed to insinuate Steven was not who he said he was and she was better off without him. She'd already guessed the first part, and she adamantly denied the latter, then told him to get out and not come back.

But where did Steven get an airplane? Why had he never mentioned it or that he was a pilot?

Authorities then located the downed aircraft in the extreme depths of a glacial lake located in a designated wilderness area in the Sierra Nevada mountains. Ballard had shown up again, this time with a smirk on his face. He'd casually informed her that due to a host of reasons, from EPA regulations down to cost effectiveness, the plane was unsalvageable. Gear from the crash had floated to the surface, but Steven's body remained underwater, probably strapped into his seat from now until time's end.

There was no turning back, not for Steven, and not for her, either. She extended the money order to the pilot.

Bobby's smudged hand reached for it as a taxi pulled

up. It stopped with a squeal of brakes and the passenger door flew open. A man hit the ground running.

"I caught you, thank God," he said as he ground to a stop in front of the pilot. He didn't spare Chelsea so much as a glance. "I need to rent that helicopter," he added. "I need to get to my house outside of Elko, Nevada. There's a private airstrip there you can use. I'll pay whatever you want. Just hurry."

Greed stole into Bobby's eyes. He licked his lips as he glanced at Chelsea and for a second she was sure he was about to send her packing. The panic of that possibility cemented the importance she'd placed on this sojourn and any lingering doubts fled. If Bobby thought he could ditch her for Mr. Money Pockets, he was in for a fight.

Before she could plead her case, Bobby turned back to the newcomer and sighed. "Sorry," he said with obvious regret. "I'm already booked. This little lady here, well, me and Gertie are all hers for as long as she needs."

The newcomer turned the force of his attention to Chelsea. Standing face-to-face with her, he appeared younger than she'd originally thought, closer to forty than fifty. His suit looked expensive, as did the gold ring on his left hand. "How much?" he said.

"How much what?"

"For you to walk away."

"I'm sorry," she began, "but—"

"How about twice what's on that check you're holding?" he said, his dark eyes intense.

"It's not about money."

"What then? Can't you see I'm desperate?"

She could see that. However, so was she.

He took a deep, shaky breath. "Listen, miss. I know this is abrupt but I can explain. I'm in the middle of a business trip, right? On my way to Los Angeles, or at least I was. Then just as my plane began boarding, I got a call." He ran a hand through his dark hair. "The bottom line is my wife's been in an accident. Apparently, it's—it's bad. I live in an out-of-the-way burg of a town. It'll take two flights and a long car drive to get me home and all that takes time. This is my only chance of seeing her, of getting to her in time…"

The pilot cleared his throat. "You two could share the chopper," he said. "Miss Pierce's destination is about halfway to yours. We could combine the flights."

"But landing and taking off again takes time," the man said. "Time I may not have—"

Chelsea interrupted. "I don't need to land. All I need is for the helicopter to fly low and hover for a minute or two while I…well, I need those few minutes and a little silence. After that, I don't care where I go as long as I end up back here. As far as I'm concerned you're welcome to share the flight."

She had at first read the guy's demeanor as dismissive or even arrogant, but now that she understood what was behind his impatience her heart went out to him. Who better than she knew the ache of losing someone you love? Maybe this guy still had time to say goodbye. Tears burned behind her nose.

"You'd be willing to do that?" the man asked.

"Yes."

He took a steadying breath. "Thank you." He glanced at the money order still clutched in her hand. "You keep that. This is on me."

"I couldn't let you—"

"Please."

"You two choke me up, you really do," Bobby said with a new grin that made the first one look anemic by comparison. "You both have some papers to sign while I refile the flight plan and then we'll be off. But I have to warn you Mr.—"

"Smith. My name is Jacob Smith."

"I'm going to have to refuel at your destination before we fly back here. You'll have to pay for the extra time and miles—"

"Just tell me how much," Smith said, waving away his waiting taxi. "And hurry."

Chelsea was happy to let the two men work out the details as she did her best not to shiver in the weak spring sun. Eventually everything was settled and she was ushered into the helicopter and directed to sit in the second row of seats, closest to the door. The space behind her was piled with duffel bags and taped-up boxes of every size.

Under the pilot's direction she strapped herself in her seat and set aside the roses. As Jacob Smith stood outside talking on his cell phone, Bobby gave her instructions about what to do when the time came to throw the flowers, then closed the cargo door and ran around the aircraft to climb aboard. She expected Smith would claim the seat next to hers, but he slipped into the front with the pilot. Given his anxiety, it made sense to her that he would want to sit as far forward as possible. She was grateful for the semiprivacy of their turned heads.

Once the switches were thrown and the blades started revolving, conversation was out of the question, although Bobby had pointed out the headset they could use to communicate once she put it on. Frankly, right then she didn't want to talk to anyone. In her mind she reviewed the directions she'd given him, taken from Steven himself when she asked him to tell her about the happiest day of his life.

He'd responded, "Today. Here with you. Now."

There'd been a long pause as she lost herself in his kisses. Eventually she'd rephrased the question. "Okay then, the happiest day before we met?"

He didn't miss a beat. "That's easy. There's this little cabin not that far from here," he'd said, and then proceeded to describe a mountain getaway in such detail she could not only see it in her head, but was also pretty sure she could find it on a map. "It was one of the last places I visited with my parents. I'll never forget it."

Once she'd finally accepted his death and the repercussions that would live with her forever, the need to somehow bring peace to her life became imperative. She'd thought of visiting the lake where his plane was entombed in water. But then she'd remembered this cabin and chosen past joy over current pain.

The helicopter rose off the ground and her stomach lurched. Ninety minutes. She retrieved the bouquet of roses, glanced at the gold foil handwritten note she'd attached to the stems and clutched them to her chest. Their perfume bathed her face as she closed her eyes.

SOMEHOW, DESPITE THE loud and constant whirring of the blades, she managed to fall asleep, but awakened with a start. Gazing out the window, she saw little but tree-covered mountains in every direction. Where were they? She put on the headset. She could see the tops of both men's heads but there was no conversation going on between them.

"Are we getting close?" she asked.

Bobby threw her a thumbs-up. His voice crackled through the headset. "We're almost there. Look down. See the river?"

This time when she gazed out the window she glimpsed the unmistakable glitter of water winding its way through the trees.

Bobby's voice came through the comm system again. "Remember to wait until I tell you to open the window. I'll get down close, but first I'll circle the area so you can check it out."

"Sounds good."

"I told you not to do that," Jacob Smith interjected.

"We've been over this already," Bobby snapped. "Like I said, this part of the flight is Chelsea's."

"You will go nowhere near that house, is that clear?"

"Why not?" Chelsea asked.

"It'll…waste time," Smith said, his voice tight.

"No, it won't," Bobby insisted.

"It's okay, do as he says," Chelsea told Bobby. She was looking for peace and closure, not arguments. "I'm fine."

Smith's grunt sounded smug. Or maybe just relieved.

But the tension between the two men was palpable. What had gone on while she slept?

Within a few minutes, the trees began to thin and a small meadow appeared, just as Steven had described, right down to the wildflowers carpeting the ground and the old rock wall bordering three sides. She sat forward as a small cabin came into focus. Bobby headed straight for it despite Smith's continued insistence that he stop. She tried to ignore their bickering. A curl of smoke drifted upward from the chimney and that surprised her for some reason. Silly that it should—Steven hadn't been here in years and hadn't known who owned it now or even if it was still here.

Broad stone decks surrounded the small residence while budding tree limbs brushed the roof. She could all but feel Steven sitting beside her, eagerly looking out the window, pointing out details, his breath warm against her cheek. Her hand pressed against the glass as her gaze swept over the meadow they once again circled. The river where Steven had caught his first rainbow trout glistened nearby.

The last time she'd seen him he'd asked her to marry him. After her enthusiastic yes, they'd made love and somehow it had been different, more profound, perhaps, more meaningful than ever before. Afterward, they'd talked for hours about the kind of house they'd build. Looking at this cabin, it was clear he'd channeled his vision from this very spot.

"Goodbye, my love," she whispered with her fingers against the glass.

"It's time, Chelsea," Bobby said. She took off the

headset, craving solitude. The chopper moved away from the cabin toward the river. Was someone inside the cabin, watching their departure and wondering why they'd been subjected to this noisy intrusion? No matter, the chopper would be long gone before anyone had a chance to complain.

She unclipped the straps that held her in her seat, scooting forward a little to slide open the window as the wind immediately whipped her long dark hair across her face. The river below flowed in endless rhythm and she pictured a young Steven, fishing pole in hand, walking the grassy banks.

Was she angry with him? Yes. He'd omitted key facts about himself, been cagey, maybe even dishonest, and that went against everything she'd thought she'd known about him. But mostly, she just felt alone and cheated and sad.

Loud voices yanked her attention back to the front of the helicopter. She could only see Bobby's face and he looked livid. A sudden jerk was quickly followed by a distinct shudder, and now they made a slow turn back toward the meadow. Her stomach rolled. In her rush to find something to hold on to, the roses fell from her grasp and slid across the floor. Peering between the front seats, she saw Smith's hand close around Bobby's wrist as he clutched the control stick. The shouting between them continued while the chopper's erratic movements became even more pronounced.

She scooted back in her seat, refastening the buckles with shaking hands. The headset slid toward the door with the roses. She hooked it with her foot before raising her leg and grabbing it. She pulled it over her ears and winced as the shouts became unbearably loud and heated.

"You just had to circle the damn house, didn't you?" Smith roared. "You idiot."

"Get your hands off me. What the hell is wrong with you?"

"Land this damn thing," Smith insisted.

"Now you want to land? I thought you were so hot to trot." There was a moment of tense silence. Smith released his grip on Bobby's wrist. A second later, Bobby swore.

"Are you kidding me? Put that gun away."

A gun!

"Land the helicopter," Smith said and now Chelsea, too, saw he held a dull black revolver and it was pointed at Bobby.

"You're going to get us all killed," Bobby bellowed.

"You're overshooting the meadow," Smith growled. "Land in the meadow."

Chelsea glanced out the window. They were moving over the trees now. Green tops swayed just a few feet below but at least the chopper seemed stable. But why did Smith want to land? Wasn't his whole point speed? And why in the world did he carry a gun?

Bobby suddenly lunged toward the armed man as though trying to grab the weapon. A shot reverberated in the small cabin, deafening, terrifying. Bobby grabbed his right arm as blood oozed through his fingers. "You—you maniac!" he yelled.

"Land this damn thing," Smith repeated as he jabbed

the air with the gun. As if sensing Chelsea's horrified gaze, he turned to face her, pinning her to the seat, his once mournful eyes now cold and menacing. Chills raced along her spine as he turned his attention back to Bobby.

The helicopter moved sideways like a flying crab, tilting slightly on its left side. A sudden crash came from behind them, immediately followed by a rolling shudder that vibrated through the metal hull.

"We lost the rear rotor," Bobby gasped.

"Land!" Smith demanded.

"It's too late for that. Get that gun out of my face!"

The chopper spun, the nose lower now, and plummeted down through the greenery as Bobby obviously worked to accomplish a life-saving landing. His labored breathing played in her headset like a dirge. Seconds passed in blinding speed. Chelsea held on to the straps, her thoughts moving from the drama in the front, to the love she'd lost, to the future now slipping through her fingers.

A microsecond later, the skids hit the forest floor and all the cargo behind her shot forward like missiles, flying at her head and shoulders and at the backs of the two seats in front of her. She had a moment to assess the fact that she was still alive and then they were moving again, this time tearing through the underbrush, what remained of the blades crashing against tree trunks, skids catching on undergrowth, branches protruding through Chelsea's open window then snapping and breaking, flying into the chopper, aimed at her. Everything came to a sudden, grinding halt. The windshield shattered as the forest invaded the front with the finesse of a bulldozer, pushing the passenger and pilot seats back toward Chelsea. The baggage that had bombarded her from behind now flew into her face, burying her.

Steven! her heart shouted as she lost consciousness without forming another cognizant thought.

Chapter Two

Adam Parish took off his black-rimmed glasses and set them aside, pulled his shirt over his head and faced his image in the mirror. The bullet wound on his left shoulder looked better than it had. There would be a scar, but it wouldn't be the only one on his thirty-two-year-old body, and at this point, who cared?

That sentiment—*who cared?*—had been his calling card for so long it had become a second skin. It had turned him cynical and suspicious—not suspicious enough as it turned out, but there was no denying his mother's sweet, trusting little boy hadn't made it into adulthood.

Except for a brief moment when everything had changed.

But like most miracles, his had come and gone like the sweep of a clock's hands and he was back to square one.

He applied a clean bandage to his shoulder and taped the gash over his eye. His short beard softened his jawline while the spikey blond hair on his head always struck him as comical. He had one week to go before he cleared out of here and then he'd—

A thumping noise outside lifted every hair on his arms. Even before he separated the blinds above the bathroom sink and angled his head to peer outside he knew what he would see. A low-flying helicopter approached the cabin from over the meadow.

Oh, no…

Within seconds, he grabbed the glasses, shrugged on his shirt, rescued his gun from the top of the toilet tank and stuffed it into his waistband. He ran to the back door and snatched the loaded rifle he kept there, then let himself out and moved to the northeast corner of the deck, where he could track the helicopter.

One thought drummed in his head: *they found me.*

He expected the aircraft to land in the meadow, close to the house. He expected an army of men to disembark, guns blazing, Holton's revenge swift and lethal.

He didn't expect the helicopter to look so ancient. It wasn't his adversary's style. Was this flyby simply a matter of a stranger's harmless curiosity about the old house or was it more than that? Had Holton employed mercenaries?

The helicopter didn't land and that left Adam relieved and yet confused. It flew toward the river, gently descending above the water, where it remained for a minute or two. Then the aircraft tilted suddenly—that had to throw the passengers around a little. He stepped around the corner of the house to see better. The chopper moved away from the river, briefly hanging over the meadow, then it climbed eastward toward the forest, its movements jerky and unpredictable.

Engine trouble? Trouble of some sort, that was for sure, including trouble for him. Even if it disappeared over the far mountains, the fact that it had circled the house meant that it was time for him to clear out. It might have been reconnaissance for a ground-based unit who even now could be advancing via the only road connecting this cabin and the nearest town. He'd rigged a sensor down at the beginning of his twisting lane. Once activated, it would beep the monitor in his pocket and he would know he had about ten minutes to disappear.

A sudden noise caught his attention and he turned to see the helicopter's aft rotor tangle with the top of the tallest tree. Parts went flying. The aircraft seemed to stall. Nose down, it disappeared into the forest. He jumped off the porch, the rifle still clutched in his hand. While his brain told him to get the hell out of there while he could, his heart said he had to see this through.

Crashes and thuds echoed from the forest. A fiery explosion seemed inevitable, but none came, just the continuing cacophony of breaking trees and mangled metal. He vaulted the rock wall and sprinted across the meadow, ever wary of a sniper but growing more convinced by the moment that what had happened was an accident and that lives were in danger.

And this meant other people would be coming, as well. Friend or foe, this crash would be investigated and that would bring killers and cops right to his doorstep.

Turn around and go back—get out of here now. He ignored his own warning.

After the full light of the meadow, the forest seemed dank, dark, secretive. He'd been away from Arizona, his home state, for more than a year now, and never more than at this moment did he miss the open desert terrain and the warm, dry air. The underbrush was difficult to traverse. His own crashing noises echoed in the dense closeness as he headed in the direction he figured the chopper had gone down. There were few other sounds.

He finally emerged into a clearing of sorts, but that quickly erupted into a battered, mowed-down trail of broken branches and flattened saplings. It had to be at least thirty feet across, lined with scarred trees and pieces of metal strewn about. The faint smell of fuel urged him forward. And sitting at the end of the trail was the downed chopper, bladeless now, the rear end still mostly intact, no signs of fire or of life.

He made his way down the newly created and narrowing path to the tail of the helicopter. As he moved forward, he saw the crumpled metal of the front of the chopper. It was about half as big as it should have been, thanks to an old growth stump that had put an end to its forward momentum.

The cargo door was the only possible way to get inside. It had jammed, though. He searched for something to use as a makeshift crowbar.

"Anyone in there?" he yelled as he picked up a branch and discarded it. Too flimsy. He continued the search. "Hello, can anyone hear me? Can you open the cargo door?"

He finally found a long piece of metal, probably a portion of one of the blades, maybe a piece of a skid. Using that, he leveraged it into the door crack and shoved. Eventually, the metal moved and he was able to slide the door half-open.

Boxes and crates filled the rear of the aircraft. The passenger and pilot seats had been pushed back. There was just room for him to step inside and almost stand. He shifted debris to clear his way to the pilot, where he paused a second before putting his fingers against the pilot's throat, but it was for confirmation only. The poor guy sat half-crushed behind the controls; broken glass had slashed his face and hands. His right shoulder sported an ugly wound that looked like a gunshot. That, however, didn't make sense.

Turning his attention to the passenger, Adam moved aside leafy branches and glass until he could check for a pulse. He detected a faint heartbeat and immediately began clearing debris, careful when he came across a two-inch pine spur lodged in the base of the man's throat. That's when he also noticed the guy had one limp hand threaded around the grip of a revolver. The safety was off. Adam gingerly reached for the weapon but as he did so, the guy's eyes opened and his grip tightened.

"Take it easy," Adam said.

The man struggled to focus as blood ran down his forehead and cheeks. He finally croaked out a single word. "You…"

"I'll get you out of here," Adam said, though he knew that was probably impossible. "Stay still."

"You're…a—a dead man," the injured man mumbled. As he spoke, he managed to raise his arm until it bumped against the spur lodged in his throat. The branch ripped free, leaving a hole big enough around to stick a thumb through. The guy's hand immediately fell back to his lap as blood spurted from his carotid artery. Adam tore off his own shirt to hold against the gushing wound but it was too late. He'd bled to death in those few short seconds. Adam shrugged his shirt back on as he studied the lifeless and unfamiliar face.

There wasn't a doubt in Adam's mind that this guy had been sent by Holton. He dug out the man's smartphone from his jacket pocket. As it required a code, he wiped the blood off the dead man's right pointer finger and held it against the fingerprint reader to get around the code, his heart sinking when he saw a call had been made to Arizona within the last thirty minutes. "Leave a number" was the only response when he hit Call. He turned it off, wiped off his own fingerprints and put the phone back where he found it. There was no reason to try to disarm the GPS system, not when the gadget was sitting in a downed aircraft with an emergency locator of its own. He scanned the guy's wallet. It held what was probably a fake ID and a little cash. He replaced it. Straightening up, Adam glanced at the pilot, but there was no way to access the poor man's pockets. The gunshot wound in the man's arm kind of cinched his position as a hapless victim in this scenario anyway.

This had to be the work of Holton.

He dug his phone from his pocket and punched in a number.

"Yes?"

"Whip? It's me, Adam." He heard the warning buzz that announced the burner phone was running out of prepaid time. "Holton found me again. I'm headed out of the mountains."

"Did the fake ID I sent you come?"

"I don't know. I was going to check today, but not now. I'll have to leave without it." Adam felt terrible that he'd asked Whip, a cop, to break the law to help him get false identification, and now it was pointless.

"Damn. Are you okay?"

"Yeah. There was a crash—the hit man is dead. This is important. Holton…he's still in prison, right?"

"As far as—"

It took a few seconds of silence for Adam to realize they'd been disconnected. He pocketed the phone and got to his feet. As he turned his back on the two dead men, a few scattered red petals beneath his feet caught his attention. The incongruity of their presence struck him. He kneeled to pick up one, pausing to smell it, its perfume at odds with the crashed aircraft and the encroaching odor of fuel.

"Is anyone else in here?" he called.

Was that a noise coming from behind the boxes?

He shifted a few out of the way and tossed them out the open door, ever mindful of the seconds ticking by. The baggage and boxes felt like they were filled with rocks.

And then he heard it again, a shifting as a body tried to find comfort, but this time it was followed by a plaintive moan.

He worked faster.

HER EYES OPENED SLOWLY. She was unsure where she was or what had happened. Her body hurt in a hundred places and for some reason, she was trapped in an avalanche of heavy boxes. Admonishing herself to think despite her throbbing head, she shifted position to ease the pressure on her legs. A groan escaped her lips and faded away.

A male voice immediately responded. "Is someone back there? How many of you are there? Can you move?"

She tried to respond but could barely hear her own voice.

"I'm coming," the man called. "What's your name?"

Again she opened her mouth, but nothing came out. Where was she, what had happened to her? She closed her eyes, her head drooping.

The man kept talking. "Stay with me," he said, "I'm almost there." Crashes followed his comments as though he was throwing stuff aside. At last he cleared her face and she saw that she was all but entombed in a small airplane. She smelled gasoline and it reminded her of something—something she couldn't name, wasn't sure about.

The man continued clearing the space as she wiped her face, smearing something warm and sticky across her brow. Blood, she discovered, as she looked at her fingers.

He kneeled down to face her. His hair was bright yellow and he needed a shave. Dark gray eyes peered at her from behind black-framed glasses. As he stared at her, his expression went from concern to shock. The next thing she knew, he'd cupped her chin and kissed her, his lips undeniably soft and gentle and yet with a stirring of something else, too. Then he sat back and stroked her cheek, smoothed her hair, kissed her forehead. "Chelsea, good heavens, what are you doing here?"

"I—"

"Oh, my God," he said as though something obvious had just popped into his head. "They must have used you to— did they hurt…? Never mind, we'll talk later. We have to get out of here. Can you move? Is anything broken?"

"I don't know," she said. "I—I don't think so…"

He unbuckled her seat straps as she mumbled. He stood and extended his hands to pull her to her feet. She was able to stand but it put her and her rescuer so close their bodies touched. Super aware of her breasts pressing against his chest, she felt uncomfortable and awkward. He seemed fine with it. "Catch your breath and your balance," he said. "Where's your phone?"

She shook her head.

"May I check your pockets?"

Was he making any sense? She couldn't tell. He frisked her gently and she felt his hand hit against a small hard shape in her jeans pocket. He plucked the phone from her person, wiped it with the hem of his shirt and dropped it to the floor. "Sorry, but this has to stay here."

She nodded but her fuzzy brain immediately went back to the way his lips had felt against hers. Why had he kissed her? Why were his hands on her now?

"You were sitting alone back here, weren't you? Do you have a handbag or luggage?"

A handbag? She looked down at the cluttered floor, fighting a wave of nausea that swam up her throat. She didn't know if she had one or not. Who cared?

He pushed aside a few things and swore. "There's not enough room in here for me to move if you're standing. Sit back down until I get outside, then walk to the door and I'll help you. Let's do it as quickly as we can, okay?"

She nodded again and sat. He climbed from the plane, reached inside and swept a bunch of crushed red flowers out of the way. "Walk over here to me," he said. "You can do it."

She stood, steadying herself by grabbing the back of the seat in front of her. Her head spun and she felt nauseous, but the sensations passed. She glanced down and to her left and found a blood-covered man belted into the pilot's seat. His sightless eyes looked blank. Her hand flew to her mouth.

"Just come to the door," her rescuer urged.

She did as he told her, mainly because she couldn't think of another plan. Gazing down at him, she paused for a second. His bloody unbuttoned shirt revealed a well-muscled chest, while the strap crossing his body was attached to a rifle held behind his left shoulder. He'd tucked a handgun into his waistband. He looked like someone you saw on a news report, a mercenary or a bandit, a man not to be taken lightly, sexy and scary at the same time.

"Are you okay?" he asked.

She nodded. He clutched her waist and effortlessly lifted her out of the aircraft. She landed right in front of him, once again standing too close.

"Steady now. Dizzy?" he asked.

"I don't think so."

"Can you walk?"

"Yes."

Unable to process the intensity of his expression, she lowered her gaze to the ground, where she found the bruised red flowers. He kneeled in front of her and plucked a small gold foil card from the ribbon that held their stems together and shoved it in his pocket. Taking her hand, he led her a few steps from the crash. She looked back once.

Not a plane, but a helicopter, or what was left of one. The image of the dead pilot's slack, bloodied face filled her head. Had she known him? Was he her boyfriend or husband or something? Then why was she sitting in the back? Why couldn't she think?

And wait, had there been someone in the passenger seat, too? She wasn't sure.

Keep moving, she willed herself as they left the path and took off into the dense forest, ripe with dark mysteries that mirrored those playing out in her brain. The only thing she was sure of was the lifeline of her rescuer's warm fingers.

Chapter Three

Okay, so where were the questions, the accusations? As Adam guided Chelsea onto the cabin's surrounding deck, he steeled himself for a barrage of all of the above, but none came. Once on the deck, he grabbed the binoculars he kept hanging from a nail under the eaves, then used them to scan the horizon and the small road that emptied into the meadow. So far, so good.

The sky had grown dark and the smell of impending rain filled his nostrils. How long did he have before more of Holton's men showed up?

He put back the binoculars and discovered Chelsea had disappeared. He found her sitting on the sofa, blood smeared across her face, hands limp in her lap. He crossed to the bathroom, where he moistened a clean washcloth and grabbed the box of bandages. As always, the glimpse of his own altered appearance in the mirror jarred him. So did the dead man's blood all over his shirt. He grabbed a clean one and changed.

Kneeling in front of her, he gently cleaned and bandaged the laceration. "You must have a million questions," he began.

She sagged against the sofa and closed her eyes. "No," she said.

"Don't you want—?"

"No," she interrupted, rubbing her temples. "All I want is to sit here."

"Does your head hurt?"

"Yes."

He got up to retrieve two aspirin and a glass of water and returned to find her staring around the room. He handed her the tablets and she swallowed them without comment. "I'd like to close my eyes for a moment," she said as she gave him back the water glass.

There wasn't time for her to nap, but how did he thrust her into action after what she'd just endured? "Go ahead. I have a few things to do." *Like pack up and get us out of here.*

He desperately wanted to know how she'd ended up on his doorstep with a hired killer along for the ride. The most likely scenario was that they'd kidnapped her and forced her into taking them to him, but that didn't wash because she hadn't known where he was. No one did. His hands itched with the desire to shake her awake and ask her what was going on, but he couldn't do that. They also itched with the desire to caress her, to tell her he loved her, that he was sorry he'd left, that finding her here was like a gift from heaven. Would she want to hear any of that? Judging from her aloofness, no, she would not. He shoved his hands in his pockets to kill the urge to shake her awake.

The fingers on his right hand brushed a hard ridge of folded stock paper. He pulled the small foil card he'd found with the flowers from his pocket and opened it, immediately recognizing Chelsea's concise handwriting.

"'My beloved Steven,'" he read. *Steven. That's the name he'd chosen when he'd relocated to California. It was the only name he'd ever given Chelsea.* He cleared his throat and continued reading. "'I think I know the location of the cabin you described the night you asked me to marry you. My plan is to drop these roses in the nearby river as a way of letting you go. I don't want to do this but the reality is you're dead. I'll never stop loving you just as I wonder if I'll ever understand what really happened to you or why that man from the government asked me a million questions, but wouldn't answer even one of mine. Sometimes it feels as though I'm grieving a shadow. Goodbye, my love. Rest in peace knowing I will move heaven and earth to make a wonderful life for our baby. Yours forever, Chelsea.'"

"Baby?" he whispered, looking from the note to Chelsea. She was pregnant?

A huge smile came and went in a flash as the enormity of this development hit him in the gut. Had the baby survived the crash? What in the world should he do?

Protect her. Protect them! That's what he should do. And right now that meant getting them out of here.

He threw his meager possessions in a box, then trotted out to the Jeep parked in the tiny shed/garage. The back was already filled with camping gear, a shovel and a chainsaw. To these he added the new box, then he went back inside to take whatever food and drink he could lay his hands on. He wiped things down and carried the perishables out to the Jeep, where he stowed them with everything else before covering the whole thing with a tarp, which he tied in place.

Small rocks separated the cabin from the riverbank. He drove across them and set the parking brake just as rain began to fall. The nonprescription glasses immediately blurred with raindrops and he pocketed them. The abandoned logging road, their only escape route, was a quarter mile downstream. The Jeep had no roof, and its engine was temperamental to say the least. It would be a miracle if it made it to the top of the ridge—if Chelsea hadn't been there, he would have left it in the shed and hiked out just the way he'd hiked in. But she wasn't up to that.

Of course, if an attack came from the air, they'd be sitting ducks, but it seemed more likely to him that ground reinforcements would show up instead. The downed helicopter had looked like someone's paycheck-to-paycheck livelihood and that probably meant there wasn't a handy fleet that Holton could summon from his jail cell at will.

"It's time to go," he said as he gently shook Chelsea's shoulder.

Her eyes blinked open. "Where am I?" she said, and for a moment, he thought the catnap had cleared her head. "Do I know you?"

There went that hope. "Kind of," he said carefully.

"I don't remember you."

"Not at all?"

Her eyes widened. "No. Should I? I mean, yes, of course I should—you called me by a name."

"Chelsea Pierce," he said.

"Then you know me?"

"Yes," he said, confused. He sat back on his heels. "Do you remember how you got in the helicopter, who the passenger was, the gunshot, the pilot? How you got here, what happened…anything?"

She shook her head and winced. "No, none of that. I don't even know who *I* am."

His throat went dry. She was talking about amnesia. He'd known she was confused but he hadn't followed that trail to this conclusion. "We have to leave," he said.

"Now?"

"Yes."

Her brow narrowed. "I don't understand. Where are we going?"

"We're both in danger. We have to get away from here right now."

She sat up slowly and his heart went out to her. He saw no blood on her tan jeans and that probably meant the pregnancy hadn't terminated. "Do you hurt anywhere besides your head?" he asked her.

"My knee hurts a little."

"How about your…tummy or abdomen? You know, where the pressure from the seat belt might have… bruised you?"

"No," she said.

He took her hands and pulled her upright, resisting the urge to hug her reassuringly, sensing it wouldn't have that effect. His gaze dropped to her midsection.

She'd lost weight since he'd last seen her, but there was definitely a small swelling that hadn't existed before. He tried to figure out how far along she could be and decided on no more than four months. He handed her the rain gear he'd set aside to shelter her from the weather and helped her put it on. "Hurry," he said with a last look around.

They walked down to the river to the Jeep and he helped her climb aboard. The rain was coming down harder now. Once he'd stowed the rifle and jumped behind the wheel, she looked up at him, her face shaded by the oversized hood, blue eyes questioning. "What should I call you?"

Would the name *Steven* ring any latent bells that might help her place him? Probably not, so he gave her his real name. "Adam." He was done lying to her.

"Nice to meet you," she said with a wan smile.

The Jeep waddled into the river like an old wrestler climbing back into the ring. Thanks to the almost daily treks along this river, he knew to stay close to the western bank, where the water was relatively shallow. When he spied a small grove of red-barked madrones, it would be time to cross the river to the opposite shore, but only until a dead pine tree signaled a pool ahead, at which time he'd cross back to the west. It was slow going, the river gurgling under the vehicle, water washing under the doors and dousing their feet during the cross to the other side. A few times he turned to look behind to see if anyone was there, or to stare up into the sky. It was during one such glance that he remembered he'd left the binoculars hanging under the eaves. Lightning flashed to the south and he counted under his breath. On six, a clap of thunder sounded to the east.

At last he found the place to exit the river to access the logging road and jerked the steering wheel to the left. The Jeep grumbled its way out of the shallow water. The tires spun on the mud before finding purchase on harder ground. He drove forward a hundred feet, then ran back to scatter forest debris to cover their tracks. It wasn't perfect but it would have to do. He ran back to the Jeep and gunned the engine.

The road was eroded and heavily rutted. He dodged the worst of it while steadily climbing. Every now and again, he'd have to stop to use the front mounted winch to pull aside fallen branches, or shift rocks out of the way, then restart their journey. During those short breaks, he listened for the approach of another vehicle or aircraft. All he ever heard was the sound of thunder getting closer.

Chelsea silently allowed him to work. What did she make of this frantic dash in the rain with a man who was a stranger to her? When would she start demanding an explanation?

And what would he tell her?

Anything she wants to know, he told himself.

From the first moment he'd seen her he'd been drawn to her humor and beauty. It was like a man standing in the middle of the desert being hit by a rainsquall. All the loneliness and restlessness that had plagued him for well over a year disappeared with the genuine wattage of her smile. For someone with no past he could ever talk about, suddenly having a future had filled him with renewed energy and that bred hope. Weeks of being with her, loving her, spinning dreams, well, that had been heaven on earth, until he had to leave without telling her, knowing he'd never see her again and that she would never know he'd faked his own death.

Just as he'd faked almost everything she thought she knew about him.

If she ever got her memory back, she'd hate his guts and he wouldn't blame her.

And now, wonder of wonders, here she was, carrying his baby and not knowing who either one of them were.

"Why are you staring at me?" she asked.

"You're very pretty," he responded.

"I feel like a drowned rat and I'm the one with the rain parka. Thank you for that."

"You're welcome. How's your head feeling?"

"Probably a lot like the tires on this Jeep."

"Hopefully we can stop pretty soon and you can stretch out."

"Hmm…" she said. Her face grew serious. "Back at the cabin you asked if I remembered a gunshot. What did you mean?"

"Your pilot had a fresh gunshot wound in his arm," he said.

"Is that what caused the crash?"

"I don't know. I doubt it. I was hoping you could tell me."

"And who exactly are you?" she asked, her brow narrowing.

He felt a vibration in his pocket and took out the monitor. Back at the cabin, a vehicle had triggered the road sensor. It would take about ten minutes to get to the cabin, another five or so to tear the place apart. Maybe they'd take a look at the downed chopper. For that matter, maybe the sensor had detected a police car or emergency vehicles sent to investigate the crash site. There was no way of knowing for sure who was on their way up the road. With any luck he might be able to see when the Jeep reached the top of this blasted mountain and he could chance a scan below.

"What's that?" she asked as she stared at the little electronic device in his hand.

"Insurance."

She shook her head, then closed her eyes. "Why are we running away?"

"Someone is after me. Or us, I guess. I promise I'll tell you more but not now."

Speculation settled on her face as she peered at him. Of all her expressions he'd witnessed over the months, this one of wariness was new. He yearned for her to look at him the way she had before. Fat chance of that right now.

"Okay," she said at last. "I'll wait."

Thirty minutes later the Jeep, as victorious as a wheezing climber, crested the hill. "I'll be right back," he told Chelsea, stopping under the trees where there was still some cover from the rain.

She wrapped her arms around herself and nodded.

He fetched a smaller, less powerful set of binoculars out of the glove box and walked into the clearing. It took him a few seconds to locate the cabin. Adjusting the focus, he finally spied a dark van parked close to the cabin's deck. A man with white-blond hair stood near it, an automatic rifle in his hands. No uniform. No bells or whistles on the car. Within a few moments, two more armed men came out of the house and joined him. They moved under the protection of the eaves, apparently unaware he and Chelsea had escaped via the river. The blond guy took out his phone and made a call while the others watched.

An instant after lightning pierced the dusky skies, an explosion rent the air. Adam jerked his binoculars toward the forest on the other side of the meadow. Flames climbed the trees where the helicopter had gone down. The lightning must have made a direct hit. One man immediately jumped off the deck and took off across the meadow, while the other two held their ground. And then one of them began a slow turn toward the ridge on which he stood. It appeared he'd found Adam's good binoculars and now he held them to his eyes. Adam immediately lowered the set he held, but not before he saw the man's lips move and his arm shoot out toward the crest, seemingly right at Adam.

Adam stood without breathing, without moving, until the need to know what was happening outweighed the risk of looking. He all but oozed backward into the shadows before raising the binoculars again.

More lightning flashed, followed by thunder still startlingly close by. In that moment, Adam witnessed the man previously seen hurrying toward the explosion now running to the cabin, presumably called back by the other two. They all hopped into the van and tore off down the road.

Adam had seen enough. They might know he was up here but he knew the low clearance of their vehicle wouldn't handle eroded roads and trails. That meant they would locate the main highway and watch for him, or at least that's what he would do in their place. So, instead of finding a nice paved highway and leaving the forest, he'd stay on logging roads until he found a suitable place for them to spend the night. His first priority was to get Chelsea to a doctor and then he needed to study a map. There were decisions to be made and in her current condition, those decisions would have to come from him.

He'd envisioned his final escape many times over the past few weeks, but he'd never imagined he'd have to drag another person along with him. A month ago, when he'd asked Chelsea to be his wife, he'd thought he was safe and in the clear, never dreaming she would wind up in danger because of him. None of that mattered now because the only reality existed in this moment—not yesterday and certainly not tomorrow.

And now it wasn't just her—it was their baby, too.

Once more he got back in the Jeep.

"What did you see down there?" Chelsea asked.

"Three armed men. I think they'll try to cut us off."

Her gaze darted around the landscape. "What do we do?"

"Stay in the forest," he told her.

She nodded, but she had to be thinking the same thing he was: sooner or later they would have to leave the shelter of the trees. Then what?

Chapter Four

Determined not to pepper Adam with questions, Chelsea channeled her energy into gripping the Jeep's rusty frame with both hands. Instead of questioning her own origins and identity, she concentrated on the few facts she knew. One, she was the sole survivor of a crash and a man she knew had found her. Two, someone had shot the pilot. And three, someone was now chasing after them, causing great fear in her heart, something she saw mirrored in Adam's eyes. Except on him, the fear came across more as anger.

She snuck a look at him, struck by his strong profile and the aura of concentration his body language communicated. Rain had flattened his bleached blond hair close to his head while drops glistened in the short beard that darkened his jaw. His gray eyes peered into the ever-increasing twilight, apparently discerning signs of trails she could barely see. But, of course, she wasn't trying very hard to see anything. For now it was enough to trust that this man who seemed capable of anything would get them through the night in one piece. She had to face the fact that her brain wasn't up to much work right now. All she wanted was to lay her head down and sleep for a week.

It appeared they were traveling deeper and deeper into the forest. Every once in a while, Adam would slow down and check a compass, but as it got darker, even that ceased. At least the rain had quit; heavy, humid air filled her lungs.

As darkness claimed the underbelly of the woods, Adam switched on headlamps but then immediately turned them off.

"What's wrong?" she asked.

He laughed softly. "What's not wrong?"

"Why did you turn off the lights?"

"They're too bright. I'm not positive how close we are to the highway. No need to advertise our location."

"Then you think those men are still out there?" she said with a quivering voice and a strong reprimand to pull herself together.

"Yes, I do," he said. He veered off the semi-road they'd been traveling and followed a gully of relatively clear land back behind a grove of small trees. When he finally applied the brakes and turned off the key, the quiet and stillness tucked itself around them like a heavy blanket. For a few seconds, they sat very still, as though waiting.

Waiting for what, she wondered. *Waiting for whom?*

"Do you see any lights anywhere?" he asked her at last, his voice little more than a whisper.

"No. I guess we aren't that close to a highway after all."

"I guess not. Let's make camp."

Camp meant lying down and, truthfully, that's the only thing in the world she desired. Her body protested as she unwound herself from the front seat, aches and pains radiating to and fro, maybe the result of the crash she'd survived, maybe caused by the constant adjusting to the motion of the Jeep navigating roads that had seen much better days. Her left knee throbbed and she limped between the dark shadow of the Jeep and the darker shadow of a small tent. Adam had erected it with an apparent wave of his hand, and was now carrying rolled damp bedding, which he dumped inside. He soon handed her a flashlight and took one for himself but it was a few seconds before either one of them turned them on.

"It's so bright," she mumbled.

He turned his off.

"Do you have any tissues anywhere? I need to find a bush."

He snatched a small tissue package from the pocket in the Jeep door and handed it to her. "Don't go too far," he cautioned, and stared down at her with a worried expression.

"I won't."

"Are you hungry?"

"No, just tired," she replied.

"Other than that, do you feel okay?"

"Kind of."

"Where else do you hurt?"

"My knee."

"No pain, you know, like inside, like internal bleeding or a ruptured something-or-other?"

She cocked her head. "No. What exactly are you asking?"

"You were in a terrible crash," he said, studying her face. Then he shrugged as though dismissing his earlier concern. He switched his light back on as he retrieved an ice chest. "I'm just trying to make sure you're not seriously hurt," he added over his shoulder. "You'll tell me if any new pain develops or bleeding or…anything?"

"Who else am I going to tell?"

"I mean it," he said. "Tomorrow we'll find you a doctor—"

"Let's take it one day at a time," she said. With that, she walked away from him, using the flashlight in spurts to make her way until she found a big downed tree and climbed over it to the far side for privacy.

Who exactly was Adam in relation to her? How did they know one another?

Or did they? What proof did she have that they knew each other, that her name was Chelsea Pierce, that one word he told her was true?

The answer was so obvious it was like a shout in a quiet room. None. No proof at all. Zero.

Her head began throbbing anew as she tried to recall every gesture, every nuance, every word that he'd said since the moment she opened her eyes after the crash. Nothing jumped out except the kiss. That had seemed spontaneous and real, but right that moment she was no judge of character, let alone motives.

But wait, how many times had he asked her how she felt, if she was bleeding, if she was in pain. Surely that meant concern on his part.

But why?

Was she being paranoid or prudent?

Either way, she vowed to also be cautious.

THOUGH THERE WAS a definite chill in the air, Adam decided against building a fire. He retied the tarp over the back of the Jeep to guard against curious night critters and early morning dew, stowed the ice chest inside the tent and shouldered the rifle. As he stood in the dark waiting for Chelsea, he grew increasingly concerned. Had she gotten lost or fainted, or was it something even worse? Had she discovered blood, was she losing their baby?

Or had someone found her, taken her, planning to use her to get to him once again...?

"Chelsea?" he called in a soft voice that he hoped would carry.

A light momentarily blinded him and he raised the rifle.

"It's just me," Chelsea said.

He lowered the firearm immediately. "Sorry. Everything okay?"

"Fine." Her voice sounded terse and tense. Well, whose wouldn't?

Once his vision returned, he crossed the distance between them and put an arm around her shoulder. "You're trembling," he said. "Why don't you crawl into the tent and get warm." He handed her a small electric freestanding lantern, hoping that as well as a little reassuring light, it would also emit a tiny bit of heat to ward off the chill.

"Sure you aren't hungry?" he asked as he followed her inside and opened the ice chest.

"Positive."

He downed a bottle of water and a handful of nuts, then opened the flap. Picking up the revolver he'd rested beside the ice chest, he handed it to her. "Do you remember how to use this?"

"Yes," she said, "although I have no idea why."

"I taught you," he told her.

"So we know each other," she said. "Explain that to me. Tell me who I am and who you are to me."

"I will, I promise, as soon as I get back from answering nature's call. Meanwhile, keep the gun with you. When you hear someone coming, I'd appreciate you checking first to make sure who it is. If it isn't me, go ahead and shoot."

"I will," she said, her voice shaky.

Using his flashlight until he saw the trail he wanted, he moved off into the dark carrying the rifle. The forest was still and quiet and, to his relief, the dim light from inside the tent seemed to disappear behind the dense undergrowth at a surprisingly short distance. He couldn't stay up guarding the site all night—his eyes already felt grainy and fatigue had started to gnaw on the fragile edge of usefulness. At some point he was going to have to sleep.

The overriding question on his mind now was how much to tell Chelsea. How much could she bear to know, and when did the out-and-out truth of what they'd meant to each other become a burden she would have to shoulder alone once they separated? Every word of the current truth had marinated in a hot tub of lies—he wasn't even sure where to begin.

Plus, how would she handle the fact she was pregnant while running for her life? Wouldn't the best thing to do be to find her a safe spot where she could heal and he could go on alone?

He thought back to that moment on the ridge—he was positive the men at the cabin had caught a glimpse of him, but there was no way they could know Chelsea had escaped the helicopter before it blew. For that matter, there had been no sign of emergency or rescue response. That meadow was the closest staging area—if someone had arrived to search for the helicopter, there would have been visible evidence of it. That meant as far as everyone currently knew, Chelsea had disappeared or died in the chopper.

He had to make that work for her and yet in his gut, he knew she was safest if she was with him.

Oh, really, his subconscious said in a snarky voice. *Is it safer for her to be with you, a hunted man, or is it just possible you can't bear the thought of losing her again now that you've found her? Maybe the idea she'll regain memories that include the fact you allowed her to grieve for you, that you left her to fend alone, maybe that's what's really bothering you.*

But his next thoughts spoke just as clearly. *You left her once and they used her. They could easily have killed her. She's damned with or without you.*

He called out as he approached the camp to announce himself before veering to dig maps out of the Jeep's glove box. His first priority had to be to get them out of this forest and somewhere reasonably safe. Chelsea moved aside as he crawled into the tent. He set the rifle in front of the flap and turned in the tight space to sit down. She'd unrolled a couple of sleeping bags and had wrapped one around herself.

"Okay," she said. "For starters— "

"Just a second," he said as he grabbed the wilderness map. "Let me check something out." He unfolded the map and did his best to locate their position. It appeared to him that the road they'd been on had emptied into the town of Black Boulder several miles before. What if they doubled back? If he were Holton's men, he would have staked out that town yesterday afternoon and perhaps moved on to others down the line by now. Scanning the map more closely, he decided that would be their best bet. The added bonus was the place appeared big enough to support a few amenities and services. It had begun to prey on his mind that he'd lost phone connection with Whip. The old guy might have been an Arizona cop for years but he was also a consummate worrier.

Adam looked over more of the map, half plotting a route east, when he recognized the town of Spur located less than twenty miles from Black Boulder right over the state line in Nevada. With a twinge of hope, he wondered if another of his dad's longtime friends still lived there. Doc Fisher could be a lot of help if he'd maintained his Nevada address.

"Are you stalling?" Chelsea asked.

He looked up from the map to find her knees bent, arms wrapped around her legs, eyes piercing. In a few weeks, a pregnant belly would prevent that position.

"A little bit."

"Start by telling me who I am."

He folded the map and set it aside. Her dark hair glimmered in the dim light as she peered at him. Who was she? The love of his life; the mother of his baby; the woman he would take a bullet for. That's who she was, at least to him.

He started with the basics. "Your name is Chelsea Ann Pierce and you're twenty-six years old. You live in San Francisco, where you run a food truck that mostly caters to business clients. You're a fantastic chef, which makes sense since you graduated from culinary school just a couple of years ago. Your parents' names are Troy and Helen. They live north of the city in a tiny coastal town called Bodega Bay, where they run a seaside tavern. You have three sisters and two brothers. Everyone lives in Northern California except your oldest sibling, Bill, and he lives in Nevada on a few dozen acres of sand with his wife, Jan, and enough guns to overtake a third-world nation."

"Who are you and how did we meet?"

"My name is Adam Parish. I work construction." That had been true when he met her and since he was still on the fence about how much to share, he left it at that. "One day, you and your truck rolled up to the building site I was working on. You made me the best pastrami sandwich this side of New York. As you were leaving, your truck rolled over a few nails. I changed the resulting flat and our friendship was born."

"Based on deli meat and tires?" she asked.

"And pickles. We both love dill pickles."

His joke didn't even elicit a smile. Come to think of it, she'd been a little standoffish since she'd returned from the woods.

"Have you always worked construction?" she asked.

"Not always."

"What else did you do?"

"I was a cop for a while," he told her truthfully. "When that fell apart, I became a bodyguard."

"And then you decided to build things."

"Yes."

"Hmm, so to be clear—there's nothing between us except friendship?" she said.

"Well—"

"That's a pregnant 'well,'" she interrupted. "We were more?"

"In ways," he said, unwilling to trot out their romance and getting wound up in details that would no doubt make her furious.

"Then why was I flying in a helicopter to see you? I take it you were expecting me?"

"No, as a matter of fact, I wasn't, especially in that company."

"You mean with someone who wanted to hurt you."

"That's what I mean."

"Why did he want to hurt you?"

This was the tricky part. *Stick to the truth*, he admonished himself. "I testified against a guy who hurt a lot of innocent people. He's in jail but he swore revenge. Thanks to the witness protection program, I've been hiding out. Now it appears he hired the bad guys to catch up with me."

"I know about that program," she said. "How could anyone have found you?"

"Someone must have ratted me out," Adam said. Someone like Ron Ballard, his supposed liaison in the program.

"So that's why you bleached your hair?"

"How did you know—?"

"It's pretty obvious, Adam. Is that why you also keep a week-old beard on your face?"

He nodded.

"And the glasses you sometimes wear?"

"Yes."

"Hmm—" She studied him for a second, then added, "Okay, so cutting to the chase, what do I have to do with all this?"

"Well, like you said, you were traveling to the cabin to visit me. By then I'd left the Bay area. They must have gotten wind you were coming, which meant you knew where I was, and they tricked or forced you into taking them along."

"That kind of makes me an idiot, doesn't it?" she asked.

He was just about at the point of throwing his arms around her and kissing her into silence, and would have done so willingly if there was a chance in hell she'd let him. He even had a picture in his wallet, so close it burned his backside, but he couldn't show it to her—he'd ruined being able to do that the moment he told her he was Adam and not Steven.

"No, it makes you a victim of this creep and I'm really sorry about that," he said. "You didn't know about this guy because I never told you. I never warned you. I wish I had. I just thought you were safer not knowing any of the...details."

"You and I weren't really close friends, then?"

"It's kind of more complicated than that," he said.

She sighed. "Really?"

"Isn't it always?"

"I don't know, I don't remember," she said, sighing. "All this aside, it sounds as though this isn't my fight."

"You're just caught in the middle of it."

She stared at him a moment and bit her bottom lip. "Are my parents the kind of people who would take care of me while I got my memory back?"

"If they were here, sure."

"I think I should go home."

"How?"

"I'll take a bus."

"Not without first seeing a doctor," he said firmly and knew the second the words left his mouth it had been the wrong thing to say.

"Tell me you are not issuing ultimatums," she said.

"I—"

"Because that is totally unacceptable. I'm a grown woman."

"I know," he said, "but it's not that simple."

"Is everything complicated to you?"

"Living is complicated, Chelsea." He didn't want to terrify her but the thought of sending her off on a bus made his blood run cold. "Without me to protect you—"

"I'll be fine," she said.

"Someone could come after you again. They'd figure you know where I was going next."

"But I won't know."

"I don't think your word will carry a lot of weight."

"Maybe not, but that's my decision."

"That's ridiculous," he said, irritated now. "How are you and your peace-loving parents going to fight off killers like Devin Holton's merry band of misfits and thugs?"

"Who's Devin Holton?"

He clamped his mouth shut. He hadn't intended on giving her a name she could repeat at a time when it could cost her dearly. "You've been acting kind of strange since we made camp," he said gently. "What happened?"

"What do you mean 'what happened'?"

"You left here a while ago and came back minutes later kind of…I don't know, touchy."

"Touchy? Okay, maybe I am. Maybe it's because your story doesn't hold water. Maybe it's because I'm afraid. Maybe it's because I survived a crash that killed two other people and I don't know who you are and I don't even know who I am."

"I told you who you are and who I am," he said.

"How do I know you aren't making it up? What proof do you have that I even know you, that my name is Chelsea and my parents are Troy and Susan?"

"Troy and Helen."

"Whatever."

"Why in the world would I lie about that?"

"Because," she said. "Because nothing makes sense.

We're only kind of friends and yet I'm flying to see you? Why would I do that?"

"They forced you."

"Then why shoot the pilot and not me?"

"I don't know."

She shook her head and winced. "Adam, or whoever you are, all I do know is I'm confused and very tired and I wish you would go sleep outside."

"That's not going to happen," he said.

"Why?"

"Because I need to be in here with you."

"And I need you to be somewhere else."

She might not recognize that tone of voice, but he did—he'd heard it a couple of times before, never directed at him, but once with a thieving employee and again with a pushy salesman. She had drawn a line in the sand and it would take a fool to cross over it. She needed space.

"Fine," he said, getting to his knees and bunching his sleeping bag in his arms. "Have a great night."

"Leave the revolver," she said.

"Why?"

"In case the bad guys find us."

"I'll be right outside."

"Just leave the gun."

"Whatever you want," he said, sorry about the sarcasm dripping in his voice but unable to curb it. He zipped open the flap, scooted outside and pulled a sleeping bag and the rifle out with him.

"Adam," she said, and he met her gaze. Her heavily shadowed eyes and fatigue sunken cheeks touched his heart. "I'm sorry. It's not fair that I keep the tent. I'll sleep outside—"

"Not on your life," he said. "And I'm the one who's sorry. This whole thing is my fault. I'd give anything if it meant you weren't in danger."

"You've been nothing but kind to me," she said, her eyes now growing bright with tears. "You saved my life."

He reached inside and touched her face. To his relief, she didn't sweep away his hand and instead covered his fingers with hers. "Don't cry," he said softly. "It's going to be okay. I promise I won't let anything happen to you. Now get some sleep, okay?"

"Maybe tomorrow I'll wake up with all my memories intact," she whispered.

"I hope so," he said, and once again fought the urge to kiss her. As he zipped the flap closed again, the lantern light inside the tent went out.

He used the flashlight to make a bed on the ground, curled into the sleeping bag and closed his eyes. If she was determined to leave him, he'd have to let her go, but somehow he'd have to come up with a way to prepare her for the return of her memories. How would she handle the moment when she realized he was her beloved Steven, and that instead of dead and gone, he was very much alive and on the run?

And maybe not so beloved anymore...

He thought of the picture he carried. Taken in front of the Golden Gate Bridge, where they'd gone to picnic, they'd stood arm in arm while Chelsea trusted a stranger with her phone to take their photo. She had printed it out, written their names at the bottom, drawn in a small red heart and given him a copy.

Every photo on his phone had been destroyed when his plane hit that lake. This picture was the one memory he allowed himself of the woman who had stolen his heart and now he'd gutted his opportunity to use it to reassure her by giving her his given name of Adam. Could he explain it away? Should he show her the note she'd written with the roses? Would it make things better or worse?

Maybe it would shock her memory into hyperdrive. Or maybe it would force it further underground.

I'll sleep on it, he decided. But an hour later, he was still staring into the dark.

Chapter Five

They broke camp as soon as there was enough light to travel back through the underbrush to the old road. Neither of them said much. Poor sleep, stiff joints and worrisome thoughts didn't make for sparkling conversational gambits and Chelsea was just glad to be on the move again.

"Is it my imagination or are we going back the way we came?" she asked.

"You've always had a great sense of direction," he said. "We're looping back to an outlet from this forest that we bypassed yesterday, headed to a small town called Black Boulder. My hope is that the bad guys decided we went on ahead and are miles away when we surface."

"That sounds kind of chancy."

"Chance is all we really have," he said. "We'll temper it with caution. After Black Boulder we're aiming for a town called Spur. I know a guy there. Well, I think he's still there. He's a retired doctor. He can check you out."

"Not again with the doctor thing," she said impatiently. "You're like a broken record. Anyway, don't you remember what I told you last night? I'm going home. If there's a bus station in Black Boulder, I'm getting out of here. We've been over this."

He glanced at her before looking once again at the road. "What if I take you to a bus as soon as a doctor—?"

"Stop it already," she demanded.

"Chelsea—"

"No more arguing. It's not just my doubts about our…relationship. The fact is you'll be better off without me to worry about."

"I like worrying about you," he said with another glance.

"Please," she said. "My mind, or what there is left of it, is made up. Let's just see if we can find a bus station."

Within an hour they'd turned west, and within minutes of that, the ruts and weeds in the road started to disappear. Eventually, road signs announcing a wilderness area ahead appeared. Gradually, the road became graded and the ride smoothed out. The engine had a new knocking noise, but it kind of blended in with all the others, sort of like a calypso band. Things were looking up until Adam mentioned their diminishing fuel supply and expressed hope that Black Boulder wasn't too far away.

They eventually found a bare-bones gas station, and as Chelsea warily eyed the empty road in front of it, Adam filled the tank and paid in the office. Within a few miles, a sign announced Black Boulder ahead and at this point, Adam left the main road and started traveling small arteries, always headed in the right direction.

They stopped when they found a larger gas station and parked off to the side. He turned back to face her after climbing out of the Jeep. "Put the rain gear on, okay?"

"Why? It's dry and warm—"

"So no one sees your face," he said softly. "I'm going to go buy some phone minutes so we can prepare your parents for your arrival."

"Prepare them?"

"By now they either think you're missing or dead," he said gently. "It's risky to alert them of your safety— I mean, they're bound to react and if anyone is keeping an eye on them. Well, on the other hand, they'll need to meet your bus if there's one available in this little town. I'll ask at the station. Stay low, okay?"

She nodded and put on the dreaded rain gear that was still damp from the day before. He was back within a few minutes. "The bus station is down the street a few blocks," he told her as he started the engine. "I'll park in the alley on the off chance they know about the Jeep and go inside to get a schedule. If there are any buses leaving this morning, I'll buy you a ticket—"

"I can buy my own."

"With what?"

"Good point. I'll pay you back—"

"Let's worry about that later," he interrupted. "If there is a bus, we need to talk a little more before you leave. There are things you need to…well, be prepared for and maybe you'd like some breakfast to hold you, or coffee or something."

"I'm starving," she said.

"Me, too. First things first—let's see if there's a west-bound bus today."

There was the slight feeling of anonymous safety sitting in a hooded coat inside a car even if it didn't have a roof. Adam eventually pulled into an alley and parked. She could see the closed back door of the bus station across the way.

"I'll be right back," he said.

She caught his hand. "Be careful, Adam. You're the one they're after, you know."

He pulled out the eyeglasses and settled them on his nose. Reaching into the back, he produced a baseball cap and shrugged that on over his bright blond hair. With his beard growth, he looked like a lot of the guys they'd passed while driving along the streets of this tiny mountain town.

"The keys are in the ignition," he said, his voice intense. "At the first sign of trouble, get out of here. The guy at the gas station said the sheriff's office is four blocks farther down—turn left, go about a half a mile. Tell them whatever you want, just stay safe."

"Adam. Don't you want to take a gun or...?"

"Not into a bus station, no. Bad idea. You keep it, I'll be right back," he repeated and walked off as though he didn't have a care in the world.

She moved over the gearshift and sat behind the wheel, eyeing the ignition key and the empty alley in turn.

BACK IN ARIZONA, before his mother was murdered, Adam often rode out into the desert alone, but he always carried a rifle. Because his father was a cop, he was familiar with firearms. They'd seemed a part of his equipment: a saddle for the horse, a sleeping bag to protect against cold nights under the stars and a rifle in case he crossed paths with a coyote or a rattlesnake and he couldn't avoid confrontation.

So here he was in another kind of wilderness, a civilized grouping of people and buildings, knowing there was a fifty-fifty chance a killer could be lying in wait. Really, he'd rather take his chances with the coyote.

He let go of that thought and concentrated on doing what Chelsea wanted no matter how ill-advised it seemed to him. Maybe there wouldn't be a bus headed west for hours. Maybe he could get Chelsea to change her mind if she had to sit around all day or, at the very least, he'd have time to explain what he could.

No need to call her parents until they had more of a plan. That call was dangerous, he knew that, because of a wild card named Lindy, Chelsea's chatty younger sister, whose idea of a secret was something you kept to yourself until the first opportunity came to share it. He'd have to make sure Chelsea understood she had to keep his name out of it.

Running had seemed like a good idea after he'd been the star witness during Holton's trial. And running with the help of the government had been interesting as well as annoying. Getting a new identity, starting over, leaving people and places behind—it really hadn't seemed like that big a deal at first.

Eventually, however, the novelty had worn thin and he'd begun to feel like a caged bird. Ballard had been his direct link and the guy was a jerk, and that didn't help. During that time, Adam had started making plans for the day he'd either had enough or someone came after him. That's the plan he'd set in motion when he got home that night and found a gunman waiting for him.

And then he'd met Chelsea and the bars on the cage had just melted away and for a little while there, he'd been more content than he had been in years.

Having Holton's man show up at his house and having to kill him to stay alive, well, that had taken massive amounts of adrenaline and focus. Escaping without Holton's paid assassins or the government knowing where he went was something of a feat of derring-do. Leaving Chelsea without a word of goodbye or explanation had taken more guts than anything he'd ever done until now. In less than twenty-four hours and with no sense of self or a single memory of him, she'd nonetheless reawakened every powerful emotion she'd originally engendered, rebuilt the home she'd established in his heart and hand-delivered a reason to figure out how to get his life back. Thoughts of watching a bus take her off to San Francisco and away from him for the foreseeable future were depressing.

Maybe he should drive her back there himself, take what time he could with her, take his chances that Holton's men wouldn't figure he'd return…

And keep her in the path of mortal danger? Risk his unborn baby? *Don't be such a selfish jerk*, he scolded himself.

He rounded the corner before making a U-turn to walk back up the block. The bus station turned out to be a narrow building filled with chairs and little else, including people. Obviously there weren't any imminent arrivals or departures planned. He walked to the window at the back, where a middle-aged woman with salt-and-pepper hair sat behind the glass, filing her fingernails. "I need a schedule for California routes," he said.

She tapped on her side of the glass with the file, directing his attention to a rack of brochures and he chose the right one. A bus left for San Francisco in two short hours. Fate was against him or for him—depended on your point of view.

He opened his wallet and bought a ticket, explaining it was for his sister. The woman seemed totally disinterested in his small talk so he shut up.

He left the building and started back the way he'd come, rehearsing what he was going to say to Chelsea. He'd find them some fast-food place where they could get coffee and something to eat and claim a booth at the back. He'd have to come clean, he'd have to man up and shoulder her anger and answer her questions and prepare her for the realization she was pregnant and alone. He absolutely dreaded it and for a second toyed around with tearing up the ticket and lying to her.

No more lies.

He was so caught up in thought that his usual sensors didn't warn him until two men grabbed him from either side, looping their arms through his and almost lifting him from the ground. Linked together, the three of them rounded the corner into the alley, Adam struggling to free himself while the men clamped his arms like vise grips. He tried kicking and yelling, but a punch in his gut took the wind out of his lungs.

"Thought you could ditch us, didn't you?" one of the men said and proceeded to jab a knife into his ribs. Adam sagged.

"Put that thing away before someone sees it," the other said, both men now all but supporting his weight. "You can do what you want as soon as we get him inside the van."

He had to rally. Once inside that van, he was as good as dead. And maybe then one of them would figure out he must have parked a car somewhere and maybe they'd figure out it was actually in the same alley as their van and then they'd find Chelsea—he couldn't let that happen.

The thought streaked through his mind as fast as a comet—she was right, she didn't belong in the middle of this. He couldn't protect her 24/7.

What would happen to her now? Even if these guys didn't recognize the Jeep and left her out of this, what would she do? Go to the police. What if she mentioned the witness protection program? What if the one who sold him out was on that team? Would they come after her?

He looked down the alley and saw the Jeep. Before he could see if Chelsea was still in it, he felt one of the men's grip lessen. Adam tore an arm free. The motion sent searing pain tearing through the knife wound. Using momentum, he swung the weight of his body around to ram into the other guy. That had as much effect as shaking a finger at a charging bull.

The next thing he knew, he'd been slammed against a boarded-up building. His drugstore glasses and favorite cap went flying. The man who had been pushed away came back with the knife held low and pointed up, positioned to gut him. Adam kicked the knife out of his hands. The guy switched to his fists, throwing one punch after another as Adam attempted to fend off the blows until a particularly sharp fist near his puncture site doubled him over and he fell onto his knees. The two reached down to grab Adam's arms and haul him back to his feet. Ready to use the leverage of his body to topple them over, Adam wasn't prepared for the sound of a gunned engine. A black blur brushed by the gun wielder, clipped him on the side and sent him sprawling. Gunfire thundered. The other man clutched his arm and retreated down the alley. The vehicle braked to a stop and Adam looked up to find Chelsea, all but invisible inside the oversized rain gear. "Get in—hurry," she said.

Blood seeped through his fingers as he held his hand against his bloody ribs. The man who'd been clipped struggled to his feet. Adam climbed into the passenger seat and Chelsea made a U-turn. She stepped on the gas. Adam spotted the thug who had gotten away—he was throwing open the back of a dark van last seen in front of his cabin. Exhaust from the tailpipe signaled the engine was already running. That meant there were three of them. The door slammed behind the thug just as Chelsea, one hand on the wheel, shot out a rear tire and kept driving.

Adam's jaw dropped open as he stared at her profile. "Where did you learn to shoot like that?" he croaked.

"I thought you taught me," she said. "What direction do I drive?"

"Just keep going southeast. Not that I'm complaining, but those gunshots must have drawn attention."

She handed him the gun and almost dumped him out of the Jeep as she made a tight right turn and sped up.

Chapter Six

"Now who needs a doctor?" she asked.

He groaned.

With one hand she groped around in the back until she found a pillow and handed it to him. "Hold it over that wound, keep applying pressure."

"We need to get you back to Black Boulder."

"Are you kidding?"

"Your bus leaves in a little over an hour. No one saw your face. We'll stop at the edge of town, put you in a cab to the bus station and you can get out of this mess."

"Adam—"

"I mean it." He struggled for a few moments to get his wallet out of his pocket and opened it with one hand. "Take your ticket and this cash—"

"Put that away," she said, not looking at him.

"You were right, Chelsea, I was wrong. This isn't your battle. If those two had known who you were or what we were driving, they would have snatched you to get to me. Now they know about the Jeep. I can't put you in danger like this. I've been selfish, just so blasted glad to have you back—"

"Have me back?"

"Being on the run gets…lonesome," he said quickly. "Everybody needs a friendly face."

Her gaze flicked to him, then back to the road. They drove in silence for several miles, seemingly at a stand-off that she finally broke with a protracted sigh. "See, the thing is, I've changed my mind about leaving. It's a woman's prerogative, you know. Now, where exactly is this friend you mentioned? In Spur, right? And he's a doctor? How fortuitous is that?"

"I'm not sure Doc Fisher is even in Spur anymore. I haven't communicated with him in well over a year."

"Listen to me," she said in her take-command voice. "We're getting close to Spur. Get on that phone and find out if your friend is still here. We need to ditch the Jeep. Call him—"

"Not until you're safe."

She suppressed a sigh when she saw the blood stain-ing the pillow he gripped tightly to his side. "Any min-ute now a very angry man driving a van or a car full of deputies who don't appreciate wild west tactics in their town are going to roar up our tailpipe. If your goal is to keep me out of jail and the bad guys from killing us, at least find out if your friend is in town. Now."

He put away the wallet and took out a phone. As he called Information, she looked around for a side road they could use to get off the main highway. When she found one, she took it and parked behind a boarded-up building that, according to a bleached-out sign, had once been Teddy's Tavern.

"Please, connect me," Adam said into the phone. His end of the ensuing conversation was terse and short.

"We caught a break," he told her as he clicked off the call. "When I told Doc we were lurking behind this old tavern, he said we're pretty close by. He's coming here to pick us up."

"What about the police?"

"They're the least of our problems," Adam said between shallow breaths. "Holton's men won't file any complaints. By the time the cops arrive on scene those guys will be long gone. Deputies won't find anything, not even a blood splatter. But this Jeep is too noticeable. Doc is driving out here to take us back to his place. He'll get the Jeep at a later date unless someone steals it in the meantime." He paused a second. "I really wish we hadn't gone back to Black Boulder," he said as he slumped.

She smoothed his sweaty forehead. "You did what seemed right. What did you tell your friend about—" she paused to gesture at their vehicle, their wounds, their predicament "—all this?"

"I just told him we'd fired shots and I'd been knifed. Doc will be here soon. Chelsea, do you want to call your parents? Your whole family must be grief-stricken. It'll take days or even weeks for Forensics to discover your DNA isn't in the chopper."

She shook her head. She'd been thinking about what he said earlier. "After what happened in the alley…well, now I can see the scope of what you've been talking about. My parents will be safer if I don't tell them. It feels wrong, but if someone is watching them…"

"I agree," he said.

"I'll make it up to them later when I can actually recognize them."

"Your memory will come back," he said.

At that moment they heard an engine. Chelsea grabbed the gun from where Adam had stashed it under the seat and tensed herself for action. Instead of the dreaded dark van, a bright and shiny red SUV rolled around the building and came to a stop. She put the gun down and stepped out of the Jeep as a man in his seventies with a white walrus mustache got out of the SUV.

"Morning," he said, all but tipping a nonexistent hat to Chelsea. "Doc Fisher at your service." Santa Claus-blue eyes twinkled as he addressed her.

"Good morning," she said.

He looked past her, zeroing in on Adam's battered face and then his bloody shirt. "Adam, good Lord, boy, look at you!" He reached inside his vehicle, snagged a black doctor's bag and trotted around to Adam's side of the Jeep. "Looks like you've still got a talent for charming the hooligans of the world. Just like your dad, huh, boy?"

"Uncomfortably like him," Adam said through clenched teeth.

The doctor looked up from Adam's wound and met Chelsea's gaze. "Why don't you get a head start moving the stuff in the Jeep into the back of my car? We don't want to stick around here any longer than we have to."

"Not the heavy things," Adam said.

Chelsea cast Adam an exacerbated look. "Good grief," she muttered.

The doctor's mustache twitched as he smiled, but his expression changed when he stripped off Adam's shirt and examined his torso. After a few seconds of closer inspection, he seemed to relax. "You say this is a knife wound?"

"Yes."

"Well, you're lucky. It's not as deep as I feared and it's relatively clean. I'll stitch it up back at the house."

As he applied a temporary bandage, Chelsea moved the Jeep's cargo. Once in a while she caught sight of the shirtless Adam and had to force herself to look away. She recalled the strength of his powerful arms when he'd lifted her down from the chopper and the way he'd stood as close as a…as a lover.

Why was it so easy for her to imagine him holding her against his bare chest, owning her with his kisses, his hands…

"Need some help?" Doc said.

She tore her mind away from fantasy and shook her head.

"I'll get the chainsaw and the tools," he insisted. "You help the boy into the car, get him lying down in the back. How about you? Are you hurt, too?"

"No," she said.

"Don't forget about your head and possible other injuries," Adam said.

"How can I?" she asked as she approached him. "You always seem to remind me."

Doc Fisher cleared off the desk in his office then helped Adam perch on top of it. "There are clean towels in the hall closet," he told Chelsea. She left the room as Doc rustled around in a wall cabinet filled with medical supplies, then spent a few minutes cleaning off the abrasions on Adam's forehead, nose and cheek.

Chelsea returned with a stack of snow-white towels. "Do you need help?" she asked.

"No, I've done this a hundred times. My wife, Val, is off playing keno but she'll be back in an hour or so. She'll call the pizza place and we can eat lunch."

"Oh, let me fix lunch," Chelsea pleaded. "Adam says I can cook. Let's see if he's right. Anything in your kitchen you don't want me to use?"

"Knock yourself out. I'll need a half hour or so to put Adam back together." He ushered her to the door and closed it softly behind her. "Are you going to tell me why she's not sure she can cook?" he asked as he turned back to face Adam.

"Long story." When Doc offered a couple of codeine tablets and some water Adam held up a hand. "I can't take those. Someone just tried to kill us. I have to stay sharp."

Doc shook his head. "I'm going to stitch that wound of yours. That's going to hurt a bit."

"Just give me a local," Adam insisted.

"Whatever you say," Doc said as he helped Adam lie down. "What's with this scar on your shoulder?"

"Old gunshot wound."

"Not that old," Doc commented as he positioned clean towels before purging the new wound with a solution.

"Doc, let me ask you a question," Adam said as he did his best to ignore the searing pain.

"Hmm—"

"You don't seem too surprised to see me."

"Well, I'm kind of embarrassed to tell you this. See, I knew you were in the witness protection program because I hounded Whip after you disappeared. He finally admitted you were but he wouldn't tell me where you'd been sent."

"He didn't know until after I left. The man I helped put away swore revenge—that's why I was allowed into the program. A few weeks ago one of his thugs found me. I ended up killing the guy and then I staged my disappearance and death. After that I called Whip."

"I didn't know any of that."

"I 'died' under another name," Adam said. "No one from the old days knew."

"I take it you knew Chelsea by then. How did she take your 'death,' or did she know the truth?"

"I thought it would be safer if she didn't know. It was hard on her."

"But now you're back together. Did you find her or did she find you?"

"It's kind of a toss-up who found who," Adam said, wincing as the first stitch pierced his skin. The local hadn't helped a lot.

"We've got a few minutes," Doc said. "Tell me how you reconnected."

Between gritted teeth, Adam explained about the cabin and about Chelsea coming to say goodbye and the subsequent helicopter crash. "I'm not entirely sure how one of Holton's men wound up on her chopper, but he did."

"Doesn't she know how it happened?"

"Doc, she doesn't even know who she is. She survived the crash, but she suffered a concussion of some kind. She can't remember anything."

"Including you?"

"Including everything. Including the fact she's pregnant."

Doc never missed a beat but a soft whistle escaped his lips. "Almost done here. So, that's why you didn't want her lifting heavy things?"

"I've been worried sick she would miscarry because of the crash."

"How far along is she?"

"Not more than four months," Adam said as the feeling of the surgical thread pulling through his skin sent shivers down his spine. "Yikes, that hurts."

"Tried to warn you. Well, if she'd suffered a miscarriage she would have told you. You haven't seen any blood?"

"We haven't even had a chance to change clothes. I'm beginning to bug her with all my questions. I was so worried she might have some kind of hemorrhage, either with the baby or in her brain or something."

"That would have surfaced by now. It's been about twenty-four hours, right? No, she looks a hell of a lot better off than you do. I'll give her an examination before you leave, ask a few discreet questions."

"I thought it might be better to tell her about the baby when I got her to a safe place," Adam said.

"She can stay here," Doc said.

"Thanks, Doc, but I need to take her somewhere

she'll be protected if armed men show up. That's not here with you and your wife. But I think I have an idea. She has a brother about eight hours from here. I've been thinking about him since she shot that guy in the alley."

"She shot the gun? I thought you did."

"Nope, she saved my skin, not the other way around."

"You really care about her, don't you?"

Adam nodded. "We're engaged, but of course she doesn't know that, either. I haven't been sure what to tell her about herself so I haven't said a lot. I was afraid if I told her every detail she'd hate me for faking my death and leaving her and she'd be horrified she was carrying my baby. I had to get her to trust me so I could protect her. I've tried not to lie…it's just such a mess and we've been so busy running."

The doctor set aside his equipment and helped Adam into a sitting position. As he wrapped a bandage around Adam's rib cage, he sighed. "I remember young love," he said as he taped it. "It's like riding a roller coaster without a seat belt." He looked thoughtful for a second, then added, "'Course, some people keep that level of intensity their whole lives—like your parents, for instance."

"I lived in the same house," Adam said. "I had a first-row seat to their 'intensity' and to Dad's temper."

"He wouldn't have hurt her for the world," Doc said, his voice very steady.

"I hope not," Adam said.

Doc opened his mouth but closed it without speaking, then finally shook his head. "Awful business, your mother's murder. I saw her just the week before—as tied up in knots as she was with that runaway student of hers, she still had time to drop by and say hello. Wonderful woman."

"I know."

Doc grabbed a prescription pad. "Thanks to the volunteer work I do, I can write prescriptions in Nevada. Get this filled. It's for antibiotics. Take every single pill."

Adam tucked the prescription into his wallet, glad to move the conversation on. "What about Chelsea's memory? Will it come back soon?"

"I have no idea. But lacking a serious injury, I do have to wonder if she's blocking something painful."

"What do you mean?" he asked.

"I'm not sure. I just wonder if deep down, she isn't ready to remember her life, that maybe there's too much pain to face."

"Pain I caused," Adam said.

"Maybe."

"No, Doc, if she's running from something, you can bet your bottom dollar it's me."

"Listen," Doc said. "Get her to her brother's house. If he can give her some peace and quiet, she might start to relax. At the very least, she shouldn't be running. If a problem does pop up, she needs to be able to get to a doctor without being shot at."

"It would be better for our baby," Adam said quietly.

"And better for you, too," Doc added.

"Sure," Adam said. But he knew the truth. Leaving Chelsea at her brother's house would be better off for everybody *but* him.

ADAM ADJUSTED HIS body to fit into Doc's well-worn desk chair. Doc had left when he heard Val come home and Adam used the time alone to access Chelsea's brother's phone number out of the short, coded list he kept in his wallet. He punched it into his prepaid phone.

"Who is this?" Bill said by way of greeting.

Adam explained who he was, which took a second because like everyone else—except Whip and a handful of others, including Holton and his gang—Bill had thought Adam was dead.

"Escaping the Feds," he finally said when Adam finished. "Dude, that's righteous. Wait, is that the truth about what happened to Chelsea, too?"

Ignoring the misconception Bill had formed on who was chasing him, Adam went on to break the news that Chelsea wasn't as dead as reports had stated. In fact, she was in Nevada and needed refuge.

"That's a relief," Bill said. "Sure, bring Sis down here. Jan and I will take excellent care of her. I bet Mom and Dad are over-the-moon happy she's okay."

"Chelsea hasn't told them. Let's just say we've been on the run. I'll explain it all when I see you, but right now, she's in danger and I just want to get her somewhere safe. And you should know there's a couple of other issues—she's got amnesia and she's about four months pregnant."

"Whoa, that's a lot to take in," Bill said.

"She'll be safe with you as long as no one knows she's there and that includes the rest of your family for now," Adam stressed. "And because of the amnesia, we're not telling her yet about the baby. Hopefully her memory will return before that becomes an issue."

"We know how to keep a secret," Bill said, his voice serious. "We won't say a word about the baby and trust me, we won't let the Feds near her."

"Er, well, we'll talk about what's really going on when we get there, okay? Your father told me you live about fifty miles outside Las Vegas, is that right?"

"More or less," Bill said.

Adam gave him the vague directions Chelsea's parents had mentioned at a family gathering when they talked about Bill and his eccentric lifestyle.

Bill chuckled. "That's the way the old man insists on coming. You can shave off forty-five minutes of road time if you turn off the main highway when you reach a wide spot in the road named Dry Gulch. Better grab a pen and paper."

Adam did as told and jotted down half a page of colorful directions. A few minutes later, they disconnected.

His next call was to Whip and the old guy answered with a sigh of relief. "I got worried when we got disconnected last time," he admitted. "Where are you?"

"With Doc," Adam said.

"In Nevada, then. Do you have a plan?"

"Chelsea Pierce and I—"

"Chelsea Pierce—wait a second, her name was in the news. They said she'd died in a chopper crash somewhere in the mountains. Was that the same crash you mentioned?"

"Yes. I managed to get her out of there."

"Is she one of Holton's people?"

"No. She's a friend of mine. Holton's people must have used her to find me. I don't know why they didn't buy into the report that I died in the lake. Anyway, I'm going to take her to her brother's place in Nevada, where she'll be safe, and then I've got to get out of the country until things die down."

"As long as you're not coming back to Arizona," Whip said.

"I don't see what difference it makes," Adam confessed. "Holton's gotten to me twice, once in California and again in Nevada by trailing Chelsea."

"But his main power base is here. I just want you to have a life where you're not always looking over your shoulder."

"I know, Whip. But remember after the first hit man, when you asked me how they found me? I've been thinking about it. There was this one US Marshal, name of Ron Ballard, a real puffed-up jerk who threw his weight around whenever he got the chance. About a week before everything hit the fan, Ballard showed up where I worked, which was pretty odd in and of itself. He made a point of making sure I noticed his new tricked-out truck. A week later, Holton's guy tried to kill me."

"So you think this Ballard guy sold you out?"

"It sounds kind of flimsy when I say it out loud, but yeah, he might have. At least four of Holton's men have been involved in trying to get rid of me. Doesn't that sound like overkill? Maybe I know something I don't realize I know."

"Like what?"

"Like, well, I don't know."

Whip sighed. "Keep thinking. It'll come to you. Meanwhile, I'll see what I can find out about that guy you mentioned, what's his name, Ballard?"

"Yeah, but don't put yourself in jeopardy."

"I won't. You're still headed to Florida?"

"Yeah. From there I'll make arrangements to leave the country,"

"Good."

The room felt empty after he hung up. Adam pocketed the phone and got to his feet, then made himself stretch his arms over his head and then bend over and touch his toes. To his relief, the knife wound didn't restrict his movements too much. As far as the pain went, he'd just have to ignore it. Every second in this house put Doc Fisher and his wife in jeopardy and increased the possibility Holton's men were getting closer.

His growling stomach reminded him it was time to eat something and then figure out how to secure another vehicle to continue their trek. Tomorrow by this time, Chelsea would be safe. That was all that mattered.

Chapter Seven

"I can't believe you made all of this out of what was in our kitchen," Val Fisher said as she nibbled on a vinaigrette salad with pomegranate seeds and toasted cashews.

"Your fridge was full of yummy things," Chelsea said.

"You can thank our daughter, Morgan, for that. Whenever she visits, she cooks up a storm. Can you imagine preferring to cook over eating at one of the casinos?"

"Yes," Chelsea said, and Val and Doc both laughed.

Chelsea glanced over at Adam, who held himself carefully. It was going to be up to her to help him, a thought that strangely pleased her. She'd hated being wounded and afraid. For some reason, both taking control of the situation in that alley and then fooling around in a kitchen had given her a glimpse of the person she must really be.

Adam seemed to sense her scrutiny, for he looked up and smiled.

"You were deep in thought," she said.

He put down his fork. "I'm sorry to bring this delicious meal down a notch, but I need to go buy a different car so we can get out of here. If those guys find the Jeep, they'll put two and two together and concentrate on Spur." He looked at Val and said, "We really appreciate your hospitality but the sooner we leave, the better off for everyone."

"I already thought of that," Val said, "Our son is in the army. You can borrow his truck."

"No," Adam told her. "I don't want anything traceable to this family."

"Okay then," she continued, apparently undaunted. "Dorrie Simpson is selling her late uncle's truck. What about that?"

"It's kind of old," Doc Fisher said.

"Old is fine as long as it's got enough miles left in it to get to Florida," Adam said.

"Florida?" Chelsea squeaked. This was the first she'd heard of going to Florida. On the other hand, maybe Florida was a red herring, just a destination to appease curiosity. Why hadn't she stopped to wonder about where they were ultimately going before this?

"He hardly drove the thing the last five years," Val said, pushing herself away from the table. "I'll just check to make sure it's still for sale." She grabbed the cordless phone off the drain board and punched in a number.

Doc Fisher cleared his throat as he met Chelsea's gaze. "While she does that, how about you humor an old semiretired doctor and let me give you a once-over, young lady?"

"That's not necessary," she said.

"It pays to be cautious after any head injury, let alone a helicopter crash," he insisted. "And I bet both of you would like a shower and some clean clothes before you head out."

"I don't have any other clothes," Chelsea admitted.

Val hung up the phone. "The truck is still for sale. And Chelsea, you're about the same size as our Morgan and I know she left all sorts of things in her bedroom after she got her own place. There'll be something in there you can have. In fact, help yourself to anything you want. She's made it pretty clear whatever she left here isn't important to her anymore."

"Thank you," Chelsea said. "That's very generous."

"Let's go," Doc said, getting up from the table.

Chelsea met Adam's gaze. He smiled and she shrugged. He'd finally gotten his way—she was going to see a doctor.

It was after six o'clock by the time the truck was legally Adam's and they'd loaded it with their gear. Chelsea looked clean and refreshed in a blue T-shirt and jeans, her long hair braided down her back. They said a grateful goodbye to the Fishers, who were off to the local casino.

"What did Doc say about your head?" Adam asked as his gaze darted down every side street, eyes peeled for a glimpse of a dark blue van with three men inside.

She tore her gaze from his fishing hat and sunglasses, both donated by Doc for the purpose of disguise. The bleached hair that had been Adam's camouflage before was now hidden. "He says he sees no sign of a concussion."

"That's good news," he said.

"He sure asked a lot of questions, though," she added.

"Like what?"

"Oh, you know. Was I bleeding anywhere, cramping, in pain, did my back hurt…all sorts of stuff."

"Well, he's a doctor," Adam said.

"True." She was quiet a second, then added, "You told the Fishers you needed a vehicle that could get us to Florida. Why are we going to Florida?"

This was a conversation he'd hoped to avoid until they were at her brother's house. "I have to leave the country for a while," he finally said. "Florida's a good launching spot."

"But I don't have any ID, to say nothing of a passport," she mused. "How am I going to travel outside the country?"

"We'll talk about that later," he said.

"How about we talk about it now? I'm beginning to read you like a book, Adam Parish. When you get all tense like this, I know you're spending more time thinking about what not to say than what *to* say."

He shot her a quick glance. "Okay then, I'll be blunt. You're not leaving the country, at least not with me. You need to get your memory back, you need to get well. I'm taking you somewhere safe. It's what you wanted this morning. Despite my misgivings, it was a good idea then and it's a good idea now."

"I thought I informed you I'd had a change of heart, that I have signed on as your designated sidekick."

He smiled. "You are that in more ways than you know, Chelsea. But today when those goons grabbed me, all I could think of was you. I'll be honest. It scared the hell out of me."

"Hmm…" she said. "So where are you going to park me?"

"Your brother's place."

"You do recall I don't remember having a brother, don't you?" she said.

"That I do. But Bill and Jan are both survivalists."

"So you figure they'll know how to protect me?"

"I know they will. As much as I want to be the one who keeps you safe, I can't right now, not when I'm on the run."

"How about your family?" she asked. "Can't they help you?"

"I'm an only kid and my folks are both dead," he said.

"Oh. I'm sorry."

He checked the rearview mirror, his nerves on edge as he watched for a dark van to pull up behind them.

"How did they die?" she asked.

"What?"

"Your folks. They can't have been that old. What happened to them?"

"My mother was killed during a break-in," he told her after a lengthy pause. "She taught high school, one of those dedicated teachers everybody loves. She'd taken a personal day off work for a meeting with my father's boss, something we found out after her murder. The car keys were in her hand when I found her—"

"*You* found her?"

He nodded. "Anyway, someone had broken the glass in the back door. I guess she surprised them by being home instead of at the school. And, well, he shot her."

"Oh, my gosh, I'm so sorry," Chelsea said softly. "How terrible for you. Was it a burglar?"

"The house was torn apart and Dad said a few minor things were missing. He figured Mom surprised the culprit when she walked into the room. A neighbor reported seeing a white male in blue jeans and a dark hoodie. That didn't narrow the field much. Despite the fact Dad was a cop, he was, of course, top suspect on the list. The department said he messed up the house to make it look like an intruder. Remember these people were Dad's colleagues. Dad felt the police department's scrutiny of him blinded them to broadening their investigation."

"The poor guy," Chelsea said.

"I know. See, the thing is that mysterious appointment with the chief of police."

"Any idea what it was about?"

"None, but the obvious conclusion everyone reached was that she was going to ask for help getting Dad's drinking under control."

"It was that bad?"

"Yeah, it was. It didn't help that Mom was involved in some situation at the school where one of her students ran off with some guy. The kid's parents had just given up ever getting through to the girl but Mom started asking questions, trying to find her and get her back in school. Dad demanded Mom stop 'poking her nose where it didn't belong.' She refused, they argued, he drank and yelled…it was pretty awful."

"Do *you* think your dad did it?"

He stared at her a second, then looked back out the window and sighed. "The drinking got worse after her death. Sometimes he'd start reliving the investigation, running through the leads that had led nowhere, the disappointments and all, then he'd segue into the good old times. Once he told me that life was just a string of choices and the trick was to be able to live with the ones you make. The comment didn't seem relevant at the time, but he died that night from a barbiturate overdose. The coroner said it was accidental, but I've always wondered if he said that to protect Dad's insurance claim—for me, you know—and if the truth was Dad just couldn't face his guilt another day."

"That's so sad, Adam. I'm sorry."

He took a deep breath. "I was about eighteen by then. It was hard…living in that house alone."

"You stayed there?"

"I had nowhere else to go. My dad's best friend and former partner, a guy named Whip Haskins, helped me out." Adam smiled at the memories. "We repainted every square inch of the place, rebuilt the attic stairs, wallpapered, installed appliances—you name it, we did it. It wasn't until later that I realized all that work kept me grounded. Anyway, long story short, I finally sold the place to a friend during the Holton trial, when I knew I was going to have to cut my losses and leave Arizona forever."

"I wish I'd known you then," she said softly.

"No, you don't. I was kind of a mess. Thought I had to make a point and become a cop, but Dad's old workplace was poisonous for me. Then I went into bodyguarding and you know how well that turned out."

"I still wish I'd known you."

He stared at her a second. No matter that her memory wasn't intact, the human being she was deep inside was exactly the same as ever: kind, loving, caring. Didn't this mean that the essence of her character was set in stone and couldn't one stretch that into believing that every feeling that had existed in her heart might still be rekindled?

Like love for him? Like forgiving him?

Adam shifted his weight in an attempt to get comfortable. His side throbbed and moving seemed to be getting harder rather than easier as he stiffened up.

"I know how to drive," Chelsea reminded him.

He glanced at her and recalled their exit from Black Boulder. "I know you do."

"Why don't you stretch out in the back and let me take over? Are we driving straight through to my brother's place?"

He'd expected more of an argument from her and in some perverted way was now disappointed she hadn't fought harder to stick by his side. Man, he was a mess, one minute wanting her safe and sound and tucked away like the jewel she was, and the next wanting her by his side, where he could talk to her, look at her, troubleshoot any problem she might have although he understood he was the root cause of every current issue that plagued her.

"There's a state park about two hours from here. It'll be getting dark by then and it would probably be better to stop there for the night rather than risk being out on the road in a vehicle we know so little about."

"Doc told me to remind you to fill the prescription he gave you," Chelsea said. "According to the road signs, there's a town up ahead. We can stop at a pharmacy."

THE PHARMACY THEY found was homey and cute. Chelsea went in alone with a wad of Adam's cash. By the time she came out twenty minutes later, she had his prescription and a Nevada Spurs sports hat.

As she walked to the car, she caught sight of him sitting with his head back and his eyes closed. He'd told her their relationship was friendly and no more, but her gut told her he wasn't being entirely honest. If he currently appealed to every female gene in her body, and under these circumstances to boot, how could he not have appealed to her before?

More likely, she thought, they'd been lovers at one time, maybe estranged now. Maybe she was more in love with him than he was with her. Maybe he'd been running away from her. Egad, was she a stalker? Is that why she'd been flying in a helicopter to see him? But wait a sec, how did she know she'd been flying to see him and not flying to flee him? How did she know he didn't somehow blow up the chopper and kill those two men?

She'd gone blindly back to accepting his version of everything and now he'd made the arbitrary decision to take her to her brother's house and she'd agreed.

"There's a puddle under the truck," she said as she slid in next to him. "I don't see a blue van, though, so I guess if they followed us they're keeping their distance."

He got out of the truck, took a look under the hood and got back in. "I think our water pump has a problem."

"That's not good, is it?"

"No. We'd better find a gas station."

"Do you think they're behind us?" she asked as they drove.

He took off Doc's fishing hat and pulled on the Spurs cap. "Nice. Thanks. As for whether or not they are following us, well, who knows? It's possible. Maybe they'll show up when we make camp."

"Something to look forward to," she muttered.

At the gas station they found out the water pump was failing and no, their mechanic wasn't working, nor did they have the part, anyway. Adam explained they would have to settle for topping up the radiator and buying a couple of gallons of water to stow in the back should it happen again. He took his first pill, then they were back on the road, hoping for the best.

Chelsea sat on her hands and stared out her window, scared about the possibility of a nighttime attack, and unsure if she wanted to stay with Adam or leave. All the strength and resolve she'd summoned to help her with the day now ebbed as the sun eked its way toward the horizon.

As the mountain terrain gave way to drier, desertlike conditions, the sky grew darker. They finally rolled into a sparsely occupied park, where they chose a spot, filled out a form, tucked a few dollars into an envelope and parked. They rolled the sleeping bags out in the back of the truck, ate without appetite, used the facilities and stopped to admire the plethora of stars in the night sky.

"Kind of nice to be out from under all those trees," Adam said after smothering a yawn.

She was quiet for a few moments and then she spoke. "Adam, this morning you said we needed to talk before I got on a bus and left. You said there were things I needed to know. What things?"

He stared at her.

"You're getting tense again," she said.

"I know I am. Okay, I have a deal to make with you. I'll tell you everything you want to know tomorrow when we're at Bill's house."

"Is my life so awful you need reinforcements? What am I, a serial killer?"

"No, no," he said, reaching up to brush a stray lock of hair from her forehead. "The truth is you're the most beautiful person I've ever met, inside and out, through and through. But you're right, I do need reinforcements. Bill grew up with you. He'll have memories of you I don't have and hopefully pictures and letters and things that will help you rediscover yourself."

She thought for a second. "Okay, I'll wait until tomorrow but there's a condition."

"And what's that?" he asked.

"Kiss me."

The silence between them stretched on as the chirping of crickets filled her ears. He finally cupped her face and kissed her forehead.

"A real kiss," she said. "I have a feeling...oh, just humor me."

His hand fell from her cheek to her shoulder then to her waist. She stepped closer and raised her face to gaze at him. She couldn't get over the feeling she'd looked at him like this a thousand times. As he lowered his head and claimed her mouth, she melted against his chest, her arms wrapping around his neck. There was a humming sexuality in him, a lustiness that shook her down to her soul. He lifted her briefly off her feet, her arms wrapped around his neck, his kiss deep and long, scorching her with its fire. When he set her down, she stepped back to collect her breath. His hands followed her retreat and she caught and clasped them in hers. If he touched her again, she wasn't sure what she would do.

"We've kissed before," she said.

"Do you remember?"

"No. But you're not denying it, either."

"No, I'm not denying it," he said.

Their heads began to drift together again. She wanted another kiss and maybe a whole lot more. Nothing else mattered. Right as his succulent lips touched hers, a car rounded the curve in the road and headlights flooded over them. Her heart went from drumming with anticipation to thundering in her ears as it kicked into stampede mode. But the car passed by them, not even slowing down, and she could see in its wake that it was a small compact, an unlikely choice for three large men.

The episode threw Chelsea back into the present. Apparently it had the same effect on Adam.

"We need to get back to camp," he said, staring into her eyes. "If Holton's guys are coming after us, we need to be ready." He kissed her forehead again and took her hand. "Come on."

Chapter Eight

"Looks like no one killed us in our sleep," Chelsea said the next morning when they both awoke to find they'd nodded off.

Adam smiled, but secretly grimaced. He'd meant to stay awake all night so Chelsea could rest... Well, as she had just pointed out, they were still alive and kicking.

As she had the night before, she insisted he lift his shirt so she could check out the wound. "It seems to be healing nicely," she announced, running her hands over his bare skin. "It doesn't feel feverish."

Maybe his skin didn't feel feverish but if she kept touching him that way, there would be blazing heat and she'd be both the cause and the solution. He found himself staring at her tempting and delicious lips, which were puffed out a little as she concentrated. Last night's kiss flared in his mind and he inched closer to her right as she lowered his shirt.

"I predict you're going to be fine in a day or two," she said.

He just stared at her. His mind was not on his wound.

"I'll be back in a few minutes," she said, and excused

herself to walk to the restrooms. He took a few deep breaths and made it as far as the picnic table, where he could watch her progress and make sure no one was interested in her activities except him. The fact his attention was focused solely on the way her hips moved as she walked was just a sidetracking fact of life.

"Snap out of it," he chastised himself.

The uneasy feeling that had been eating at him since the day before returned. Where were the thugs? If he'd been determined to follow someone, he'd have waited near the on-ramp to the only highway leading out of town. Had they been lurking there and just hadn't recognized him behind the wheel of the truck? It was possible. They had changed cars and he'd been wearing Doc's old hat.

It was a chilly morning made chillier by the fact that this was the last day for an unknown length of time that he would see Chelsea. The kiss last night had opened the doorway for him to explain the true scope of their relationship. Soon. With her brother to support her, Adam would tell her about their baby. She had to know and he had to be the one to tell her. After that he'd leave to draw danger away from her and then once he had resettled, he'd get word to her and it would be up to her what she did next.

The whole thing was fraught with multiple opportunities for disaster, but at least she wouldn't be alone. Bill would know how to reconnect her to her parents and then when her memory came back—well, that's when the true decision making would start.

That was the plan, anyway.

He looked up to see her approaching and his heart did the clichéd thumping in his chest. "I'm starving," she announced as she stopped a few feet in front of him.

"Is there anything to eat in the icebox?" he asked.

"Not really. How about we go to a real live restaurant?"

"Why not?" he said.

Breaking camp consisted of putting more water in the radiator and climbing into the cab. Fifteen miles later, they came across a dusty little town named Fiddlestick with a one-stop convenience store/gas station/post office/restaurant all housed in a single rambling building.

The inside was bustling with what appeared to be regulars. No one looked suspicious, although almost all conversations paused as the two of them walked through the door.

"Looks like you order at the counter," Chelsea said. "I still have a little bit of the money that you gave me. I'll get breakfast."

"I'll have the usual," he said, and then smiled at her expression. "Yes, we've eaten together before and, yes, often enough that somewhere in your pretty head you know what I like. Order me black coffee and a bacon-and-egg breakfast sandwich. You always order an everything bagel with light cream cheese."

"Always?"

"In my experience, yes. I guess we each have our habits. I'll go scout out a table."

Breakfast was delivered fast, and was hot and tasty. As they sat at a small table, surrounded by babbling strangers and laughter, the air full of delicious smells, Adam felt whisked back to the months in Frisco. Chelsea loved eating out and with her, he'd discovered the joy of being alone, together, in a crowd to the point that this interlude struck him as not just ordinary, but extraordinary. He suddenly wanted that carefree life back with a vengeance. He cautioned himself not to get complacent. No matter how tired he was of running, he couldn't stop, because Holton wouldn't.

Filled up and ready to tackle the next several hours of driving, they got back in the truck and headed south.

After months in San Francisco's foggy, cool climate and then weeks underneath trees, the open skies of the desert aroused a host of fond memories for Adam. Even the colors were familiar: sage-green foliage, earth a dozen shades of tan, distant purplish mountains, faded blue skies.

But the driving soon became monotonous. With no air-conditioning, they rolled down their windows so air could blow through the cab, billowing their clothes, rustling their hair.

"This road just keeps going on and on and on," Chelsea eventually said. She'd propped her feet against the dashboard and extended one arm through the open window. Her head rested against the seat while windblown strands of loose dark hair flew across her cheeks. She looked absolutely wonderful. The monotony he'd been feeling fled at the sight of her blue eyes trained on his face.

Another hour passed before he finally spotted a sign that read Dry Gulch 2 Miles.

"Here's where we fill the tank and turn right," he announced as he pulled into the town's sole gas station.

After a quick stop, they drove off and it rejuvenated both of them to be off the main highway for the simple reason that this road wasn't as flat and straight. Eventually they rolled up to a stop sign, where another road crossed. This had to be four corners. He turned right and Chelsea ticked off the different steps Adam had jotted on some scrap paper. They made all of Bill's twists and turns until they found themselves approaching a barn with a giant painting of a beer bottle on the side.

"Eleven more miles," Chelsea said.

"And then what?"

"A gulch, a fence, then Bill's property. Follow the road until you hit a slight rise covered with mesquite trees. From there we can see his place." She looked up from the paper. "Or so it says here. I'll believe it when I see it."

The road, which had been steadily deteriorating, began to show signs of more frequent use as No Trespassing and Private Property signs expressing various levels of threats and *or elses* began to show up nailed to fence posts and random trees. There was a lot of barbed wire present as well, and a gate that had been pushed aside and left open for what appeared, judging from the sandy earth currently blocking its path, to have been a season or two.

"Give me a crash course in my brother," Chelsea said as they passed a sign warning the federal government that the land was protected by patriots.

"He's a little on the aggressive side of privacy," Adam said diplomatically. "He believes in the rights of citizens to bear arms and protect themselves against any and all contingencies that threaten their sovereignty. In other words, he and his wife, Jan, take care of themselves and brook no interference. And they distrust the government."

"I see. So, how do you two get along?"

"I've never actually met him."

"What? I thought you knew him. I thought *he knew you*!"

"You and I have only known each other a few months," he explained. "We were going to go visit him…we just never got around to it."

She turned a puzzled expression in his direction. "Since when do casual friends travel hours and hours to visit each other's families?"

He started to stammer something and she waved him off. "I know, you'll tell me later."

"You and Bill," he added, hastening to move the conversation along, "have your political differences, but as far as I could tell, you adopted a live-and-let-live policy toward each other. And you should know that he didn't hesitate offering to give you sanctuary and protection."

"That's nice. How long will you stay before you leave?"

He glanced at the dashboard clock. It was early afternoon. "Until you're comfortable with your brother and his wife. Then I'd better go."

"Okay," she said, her voice noncommittal, as though she wasn't sure if she resented him leaving or couldn't wait to be out from under his wing. He guessed it was a little of both.

They finally found a scattered copse of mesquite trees topping a small hill. Adam stopped the truck and got out. His first order of business was to fill the radiator with water, then he joined Chelsea under the meager shade of the trees to peruse the compound down below.

He counted three barns, a double-wide trailer, what looked like a cinderblock outbuilding and a covered shelter surrounding a pasture that housed two goats, two cows and a horse who lurked under the shade of the only tree. Chickens roamed about in another pen and half a dozen vehicles of various configurations were scattered throughout. A small garden grew close to the house. A covered well sat next to that, complete with a hand pump and a trough. A static windmill crowned the bucolic scene.

"You're right. They are the self-sufficient type," Chelsea said.

"Well, they are out in the middle of nowhere," Adam agreed. "I bet their nearest neighbor is literally miles away."

At that moment, a man wearing dark jeans and a white shirt walked out of the double wide, looked up the hill and waved an arm, as if gesturing them to come on down.

"Is that him? Is that Bill?"

All Adam could tell from that distance was that he was blond and big, which matched the picture of Bill he'd seen in Chelsea's parents' home. "I believe so," he said.

Adam waved back at the man. As Chelsea turned to retrace her steps to the truck, she called over her shoulder, "It's time to meet the family. You coming?"

He glanced once again at the double-wide, but Bill had apparently gone back inside, probably to alert his wife that their visitors were here. He turned to the truck to find that Chelsea already sat in the passenger seat, a smiling, hopeful expression on her face.

It hit him hard—her only reality was the loss of identity, including her family, her background and relationships. He'd done nothing but drag her miles away from a crash he'd admitted she never would have been in if it hadn't been for him. She'd be crazy to not want to reconnect with real people who could prove who they were.

That trailer and the people inside it represented the future to her and until her memory came back, he made up little more than forty-eight hours of her past. It was time to get this over with.

CHELSEA PUSHED ASIDE the sadness that the thought of Adam leaving her behind created—there was no point in dwelling on it—and instead concentrated on finally getting some answers, both from her brother and from Adam. What she might learn about herself was scary but she was ready for just about anything.

They pulled up right beside a short flight of stairs that led into the aproned trailer. It was apparently the back door to the place, but as it was open, it seemed the place to start. Adam parked alongside a truck that looked even older than theirs. It sported a gun rack in the back window, complete with two rifles. A prominent bumper sticker dominated by a pair of puckered red lips read Kiss My Arsenal.

She waited for Adam to join her and preceded him up

the stairs. She kept expecting her brother and his wife to emerge from the trailer, but something must have demanded their attention. She and Adam walked inside and then paused. They were standing in the kitchen. A narrow doorway occupied the left wall. Adam called out, "Bill? Jan?"

They heard a sound coming through the doorway that led to the rest of the home, but no accompanying voices. Chelsea walked toward the inner door and moved into a darkish combined dining-living area. Closed drapes explained the gloom. The only light came from a skylight in the ceiling, and strapped into a chair situated under that beam of light sat a bound-and-gagged man. Behind him, piled high, were several cartons of weapons.

Adam immediately drew his handgun and turned on his heels. Where was the guy who'd signaled at them? Chelsea hurried to the man's side. He was a large guy with dark blond hair and a very bushy, curly beard. He wore faded denim overalls and a yellow T-shirt.

"Start with the gag," Adam urged as he joined her. "We have to know what's going on."

She loosened the man's gag and pulled it from his mouth. "They've taken Jan," he blurted out. "Did you see her outside?"

"Are you Bill?" Chelsea asked.

"Oh, gosh, yeah, sis, I'm your brother and Jan is my wife. Did you see her?"

"No," Chelsea told him. "You don't know where she is?"

"They won't tell me. They only kept me alive in case they needed bait. God knows what they've done to her."

"Who are they?" Adam demanded as he brought out a pocketknife and began slicing through knots. His voice sounded like he dreaded the reply.

"I figure they're those Feds you told me about. Man, you must have really pissed them off."

"Not Feds," Adam said. "But you don't know them at all?"

"Never seen them before."

"Did they say who they were working for?"

"No."

"How many of them are there?"

"Three. One's got a bad arm, though. Mean SOB."

Adam swore as he and Chelsea exchanged looks.

"How did they find us?" she whispered.

Adam shook his head.

Bill looked contrite as he met Adam's gaze. "I know you asked me not to tell anyone you were coming here, but I've got to admit I called Mom and Dad and I suspect they told the rest of the family. I had to let them know Chelsea was okay."

"When did these guys show up?"

"Late last night. One took Jan away while the other two tied me up and then they took turns guarding me and waiting for you two to get here. They kept talking about how to make it look like a bunch of weapons exploded, like they wanted it to look like some kind of ingrown mishap that turned into a death trap, and not cold-blooded murder. Those boxes behind me are full of weapons. No ammunition, though."

"We saw a big, blond man outside," Chelsea said. Glancing up at Adam, she added, "He must have been the driver in the alley." She untied the last knot on Bill's wrists but jerked when the sound of hammering on the kitchen door sounded through the metal structure.

Adam had now cut through the bindings on Bill's ankles and the shaken man stood up. Hours in restraints had taken their toll and he almost tumbled over. Chelsea caught him as Adam ran into the kitchen to check out the noise. Chelsea scurried to the door next to a small fireplace.

"Don't open that," Bill said.

"Why not?"

"Because they rigged it to explode if it opens from the inside."

"The kitchen door has been nailed shut from the outside," Adam said as he strode back into the dining area. He gestured at the front door. "What about that one?"

"Can't use it," Chelsea said. She looked at her brother. "Is there another one?"

"In the bedroom," Bill said, pointing behind him. "But I heard banging back there, too. There's another way—unless they found it." He took a few unsteady steps, found his legs and dashed down the short hall, with Adam and Chelsea close behind.

Adam found the door Bill mentioned and tried to open it, but Bill was tugging on the big bed that occupied the middle of the room. "You guys help me push this thing against the wall," he muttered. As Chelsea gripped a bedpost, they heard breaking glass. A second later an explosion caused the whole structure to shake and a second after that, smoke made its way to their noses.

Chelsea darted back to the living room. The opaque window set into the front door was now just shards of glass, broken by the bomb they'd thrown into the trailer. She started coughing as flames raced up the drapes. For a second, she couldn't look away from the fire.

"Chelsea!" Adam yelled.

Eyes now watering, she grabbed a throw rug and beat out the flames, then ran back down the hall to the bedroom.

"There was a fire—" she began.

"Are you all right?" he interrupted with a concerned glance.

"I put it out, but it looks as though they're trying to burn the trailer down with us inside it." Her announcement was followed by more cracking glass and another explosion.

"We have to break a window and take our chances outside," Adam told Bill. "Maybe I can pick off one or two—"

"Hang on, one more shove," Bill said. "Those goons took all my weapons, but maybe they missed the knife in the false back of the top drawer. Check for it, Chelsea."

She wedged herself between the bed and the chest and pulled out the drawer. Socks flew everywhere as she emptied the drawer to find the fake back still in place. Sheathed knife in hand, she turned into the room. Bill was now on his hands and knees where the bed had once stood. Adam had crossed to the window, which had shattered thanks to the reverberations of the other explosions. He fired into the yard, taking a second to look over his shoulder as Bill yelled.

"Give me the knife—hurry," Bill said as yet another breaking window somewhere near the kitchen signaled another bomb. By now, the trailer was filled with acrid smoke and the sound of crackling flames. They were all coughing and gasping as noxious fumes polluted the air.

Bill sliced the carpet in four quick strokes, revealing a wooden hatch built into the floor. He pulled on the attached ring and lifted a hinged lid. "If they haven't found the exit, we'll be safe," Bill said.

Adam suddenly backpedaled across the room and out into the hall as a projectile sailed through the window. It landed by his feet and he kicked it down toward the living room.

"That was a hand grenade," he said.

Bill dropped into the underground passage, pulling Chelsea after him. Adam's shoe hit her head as he followed. He pulled the trap door closed right as the grenade exploded down the hall. The cramped space became pitch-black.

A light caught Chelsea in the eyes. When she could see again, she found Bill had donned a miner's cap with a bulb attached to the crown. "There's no headroom, you'll have to crawl. Follow me," he said. "Don't stop for anything unless you hear a rattler."

Did he mean there could be a rattlesnake in this tunnel? Chelsea swore under her breath. Apparently, she was afraid of snakes, and for a second she froze.

An explosion in the room they'd just left loosened dirt in the tunnel and suddenly, snakes seemed like the least of their worries. With gentle prodding from Adam, she scrambled to crawl after Bill.

No one spoke as they concentrated on getting as far away from the trailer as possible. Eventually Bill stopped. There was enough space above his head for him to get to his knees and push up on another hatch. Dim light flooded inside, along with straw and the smell and squawk of chickens. Bill heaved himself out, then reached down to help the other two.

They'd arrived in the enclosed portion of a large chicken coop. Chelsea saw the wire cage part through the open door, as well as smoke and flames coming from the trailer they'd just escaped, and wondered how in the world they could walk out into the open and not get blown off their feet.

Her brother was several steps ahead of her. He pulled on what at first glance appeared to be a solid piece of the nesting structure, but turned out to be a lever that opened a gap in the stone wall located at the back of the coop. Lights immediately turned on in the adjoining space. "Come with me," Bill said.

This time the door closed behind them, leaving them in jarring silence, and they were standing in what appeared to be a communication center. There was a steel door built into the far wall. Bill grabbed the controls for a radio. "I'm calling for help," he said. "And then I'm going to find Jan and then I'm going to take care of those damn Feds."

"These guys aren't with the government," Adam said. "You misunderstood me. They're hired guns. The fact they aren't very good at what they do is just plain dumb luck."

"They're still going to be dead," Bill said.

Chelsea moved to the door. "Where does this lead?"

"The back of the horse barn."

"Do you have any idea where they'd take Jan?"

He almost threw up his hands. "She could be anywhere. There are a million places to hide…somebody."

He busied himself on the radio, his words when he connected hushed and urgent. As soon as he put down the radio, he unlocked a cabinet and started selecting guns and ammo.

"The police are coming?" Chelsea asked hopefully as Bill shoved a loaded rifle in her hands.

"No cops," Bill said.

"But we need help—"

"Not the cops. I called friends."

"I hope they know what they're doing," she said.

"They know. We've prepared for this kind of situation."

Adam handed her the revolver. "Tuck this away," he said and kissed her forehead before crossing to the steel door. "How do we open this? We have to know what's going on outside."

Bill unlocked and opened the heavy door. Leaving the soundproofed communications room for the barn, they were once again bombarded by explosions. The animals in the corral bleated and whinnied as the crackling roar continued. Bill and Chelsea ran toward the front of the barn.

Out in the yard, two of the men hovered over a box

of hand grenades. As Chelsea watched, one of them plucked a bomb from the box and pulled the pin. He threw it at the trailer. Seconds later another explosion sent the terrified animals racing around the corral.

"They've got to be dead by now," one of the men said. He wore a bandage around the bulging muscle in his left arm. He must be the guy Chelsea shot in the alley.

"We've got to be sure," the first one grumbled. "We'll catch hell if Parish escapes again."

"How many grenades does it take to kill two guys?" the injured one protested. "I say we go look for bodies and get out of here."

"This isn't a democracy," the first one replied. "We do what we we're told."

"If we could just shoot them—"

"No bullets, you know that. Now, clam up."

As the two men continued to argue, Bill motioned for her to stay where she was as he crept out of the barn and took up a position behind a steel water tank. She couldn't imagine his new location gave him a clear shot of anyone, but it would provide protection against an explosion. There was no sign of Bill's wife or of the blond guy, either, for that matter, and in her mind, that made shooting anyone risky.

On the other hand, the killers had talked about there being only two men in the trailer. Was it possible they didn't know she was there, too? Could she use that to their advantage?

"Look what we got here," a deep voice said as an arm the circumference of a well-fed boa constrictor circled Chelsea's neck. Every cell in her body jumped to attention as his free hand grabbed the rifle from her hands. She immediately tugged at his stranglehold but he shook her off like a gnat.

His arm still clamped in place, he propelled her ahead of him toward the other two men. Where had he come from? Had she been so busy assessing what was going on in the yard that she hadn't heard someone roughly the size of a refrigerator approach her from behind?

She tried frantically to turn her head to scan the interior of the barn, desperate to find out what had happened to Adam.

Was he still alive? What else had she missed?

Chapter Nine

Adam threaded his way through the dark barn, searching for an alternate exit and knowing Chelsea and Bill would need back up.

He heard a creaking noise to his left and stepped behind several bales of bedding straw. He crouched down, all but holding his breath. From that position, he saw dusty loafers descend a ladder, followed by a tank of a guy wearing a white shirt and crowned with white-blond hair. The man was whistling a jaunty tune under his breath. Adam would have shot him right that moment just because he dared to whistle while attempting to obliterate innocent people if a shot wouldn't have made things worse.

The guy moved off to the front of barn. Was it possible he'd stashed Jan up in the loft? What better place? But Chelsea and her brother might be in trouble—he debated what he should do for twenty seconds, then scampered up the ladder, emerging in a small closed space filled with lockers and boxes.

He tore open the door to spaces big enough to cram a

human being inside, but there was no sign of Jan having ever been up here. All he found were more munitions.

When Bill and Jan had built their homestead, they'd obviously thought in terms of defending their turf. That meant that from the vantage point of this open loft, the road leading toward the mesquite trees and the back entrance, as well as the one leading away from the yard and the front of the trailer, were highly visible so that any incoming vehicles could be dealt with. But it also meant that Bill's soon-to-arrive friends would be vulnerable.

The killers had to realize this—that must have been why the blond guy was up here. Ignoring a burning desire to check on Chelsea, Adam sidled up to the platform's bulwark and chanced a peek down to the yard. His attention was immediately drawn to the two men standing over a box of hand grenades. He was just in time to see one of the men pull a pin, wait until the count of three to lob a grenade into the trailer. Adam recalled the earlier delay that happened in Bill's bedroom, when the gap between deployment and explosion had given Adam time to kick the threat away. Apparently the man had learned to wait a few seconds before throwing.

The trailer was understandably crumbling under the onslaught and several fires had started. Black smoke circled skyward but was there anyone within miles to see and report it? Adam wasn't sure why they were still lobbing hand grenades unless it was to be certain nothing remained intact…and that the survivor rate was zero.

The man who had stood by while the grenade had been thrown now waved his arms and shouted as a heated argument erupted. The combined noise of crackling fire, panicking animals and small explosions made hearing every word impossible.

Where were Chelsea and Bill?

Adam scanned the yard and almost decided they were both still inside the barn, when he spied movement off to his left and watched as Bill slithered from behind the water tank to the cover of a small building. He was inching, it appeared, his way closer to the center of the yard and a clear shot.

Adam lifted his rifle. He was ready.

Another movement caught his attention as the blond he'd seen minutes before came from inside the barn. He pushed a raven-haired woman in front of him—Chelsea. Adam swore under his breath and lowered the rifle. A bullet through the guy's back would go right through Chelsea, too.

The guy shoved her toward his cohorts, one of whom was glued to his cell phone, then stopped several feet away and yelled at them to shut up. He trained Chelsea's rifle on her heart and bellowed toward the trailer. "Parish? Is this little gal with you? Get out here, tough guy. The party's over."

Adam's gaze darted to Bill, who now held his rifle on the blond guy. The yard seemed to attain a moment of pure silence as though a vacuum had sucked up every sound, from fire to exhaled breath. Everyone appeared caught in a moment of inertia. Even the guy with the phone fell silent.

And then Bill shattered it all with gunfire. The blond guy fell to his knees. As he shifted his rifle to return fire, Chelsea pulled the revolver from under the hem of her shirt and got off a shot. The blond's bullet went wild as he toppled over onto the sandy earth.

The other two men each grabbed a grenade and spun around, aware now that the threat came from the barn and the yard itself, not the trailer. As one of them pulled the pin, Adam saw Chelsea race for the cover of the water tank. Once she'd attained cover, he pinpointed the grenade in his sights and pulled the trigger.

The resulting explosion blew both men to smithereens. Bill staggered from his position, looking dazed but unhurt. Chelsea got to her feet, revolver still drawn. Even from that distance he could see her hand shake as she perused the devastation in front of her.

Bill ran to the blond guy, demanding to know where Jan was, but the man was motionless, staring up at the clear sky, taking Jan's whereabouts and the identity of the man behind this mayhem with him into death.

Adam made his way down the stairs and out into the yard, where Chelsea flew into his arms.

"It's over," he said, holding her as tight as he dared.

But, of course, it wasn't. Where was Jan?

BILL'S BUDDIES SHOWED up soon after. For a few minutes, everyone just stood, kind of dumbstruck, their gazes darting between one disaster to the next as though uncertain how to clean up the nastiest mess of human flesh and twisted metal any of them had ever seen.

Bill left it to Adam to explain what had happened.

He decided to tell them everything he knew. The memory of one of the killers on his phone plagued Adam. Who had the man called and how much had he said? Certainly whoever was behind this knew for sure about Chelsea now, and also about this standoff. These people had to understand that they must remain vigilant.

The time for explanation was short, however, as everyone's overriding concern was what had happened to Jan. Bill quickly divided people into teams because of the number of buildings scattered across the property that would all need to be searched. He hadn't seen his wife since she'd been taken out of the trailer the previous night, and though he wouldn't say it, Adam could see as the minutes went by and people reported finding nothing, that Bill was beginning to believe they'd killed her and buried her body in a sandy grave.

It was Adam who stumbled across an old abandoned well located out beyond the pasture. He shined his flashlight down the shaft for a cursory check and couldn't believe it when he saw a mop of red curls atop a small crumpled body at the dry bottom. He yelled Jan's name, which caught the attention of everyone nearby, and they all came running. She didn't respond—from that distance, there was no way to tell if she was dead or alive.

The rescue went surprisingly smoothly. Bill insisted on being the one lowered to his wife. A few tense moments were followed by a shout that brought tears to those waiting at the top. "She's alive," he yelled.

He was hauled up and a man Bill introduced as Tang,

an aging Vietnam vet and former medic, went down with some rudimentary first-aid equipment.

"A broken ankle, dislocated shoulder and a bunch of scrapes from the fall," Tang announced once they'd rigged a harness and brought Jan to safety. "Plus she's been down there awhile so she's dehydrated."

Bill couldn't take his eyes off his wife's battered face or release his grip of her hand.

"I thought I was a dead duck," she whispered as Bill held a cup of water to her lips. She looked around at everyone, her gaze sliding past Adam and resting on Chelsea. "Some welcome we offered, huh?"

"I'm just so sorry about your home and your leg and—"

"All that can be rebuilt and fixed," Jan whispered.

"You should go to a hospital," Chelsea added.

Jan smiled. "No, honey, no institutions for me. There's work to be done here and Tang can patch me up just fine, can't you, Tang?"

"I can set the break, no problem," the former medic said as he scratched his salt-and-pepper beard. He gestured back at the gutted trailer and bombed-out yard. "But wow, your house! Bill, what are you going to tell the authorities?"

"Nothing," Bill said.

"But—"

"But nothing. You know as well as I do that once the law gets involved, I might as well hand over my land. Those three murdering scumbags never did one ounce of good in their lives. Now they'll fertilize a few tumbleweeds."

Chelsea stood closer to Adam. "Do you think he can get away with it?"

"He might," Adam said. "Technically, I killed two of the guys."

"And I killed the other one," Chelsea said.

"I'm not anxious to try to explain any of this to anyone, are you?"

"No. But you have to wonder what the people who hired those men are going to think happened to them. Will they look for them? Don't killers have families who ask questions? I don't know, it just seems impossible that three lives can be erased without someone somewhere caring."

"Let's help clean up this mess and get out of here," Adam said.

She sighed. "So much has been destroyed. They have a lot to rebuild."

Adam nodded. He didn't add what Chelsea obviously knew. Any pictures or mementos of her that her brother once possessed were now gone. Bill might provide a story or two, but any concrete proof she had of who she was no longer existed, at least not here.

"Sorry I called the folks," Bill said while the medic worked on Jan and a contingent of others went to fire up the backhoe to dig a mass grave.

"It's not your fault," Adam said.

"Sure it is. I told them to keep it between the two of them, but Mom probably confided in Lindy."

"Who is Lindy?" Chelsea asked.

"I keep forgetting you don't remember things," Bill said. "Lindy is our gossipy twenty-one-year-old sister.

Put a beer in front of her, set her on a pub stool and off she goes. If anyone wanted to know anything about you, all they'd have to do is stick close to Lindy."

Adam shook his head. "My friends knew I was coming here, too, Bill. I told both Doc and Whip."

"Would they be behind something like this?" Bill asked.

"Not consciously, not any more than Lindy would be," Adam said. "I can't guarantee one of them didn't mention our coming here to someone else, but it seems unlikely."

Bill sighed. "Either which way, this isn't a good place for Chelsea."

Where was a good place? Adam wondered. Hell if he knew. He glanced at what was left of the truck he'd bought the day before. It had suffered right along with the trailer. They were going to have to hitch a ride or hike out of here. And how long would it be before Holton thought of another attack plan from his prison cell? The only good thing Adam could think of was that no one would know where they were once they left this property. No talkative sisters or suspicious US Marshals—no one. That should provide some margin of safety.

"I have all the help I need," Bill said, and then turning to Chelsea, he added, "Will you go see how Jan is doing?"

"Of course."

As she moved away Bill dug in his pocket, withdrew a key and handed it to Adam.

"What is this for?" Adam asked.

"Jan's old van. She wants you to have it. It's got Montana plates and is registered to her under her maiden name so no one will connect it to you."

"I can't—"

"I want you to get my sister out of here," Bill interrupted. "Take her far away. That's what Jan and I both want, and before you get all dewy-eyed about our generous gift, you should know the van has almost three hundred thousand miles on it and burns oil like there's no tomorrow. Take it. Go before we dig the grave and… well, Chelsea doesn't need to see that."

"No, she doesn't," Adam agreed.

"Car number three," Chelsea said as they drove away from her brother's property.

The creaks and groans, to say nothing of the tired shocks, gave the green van the aura of a carnival ride.

"You know what they say," Adam told her. "Third time's the charm."

"Where are we headed?" Chelsea asked when they hit the main highway two hours later.

"I'm not sure," Adam said. "Up until now, my priority has been to get you someplace safe and then disappear."

"My parents—"

"Really?" he interrupted with a swift glance her way.

"No," she said. "There's no point in going there."

"Bill called your folks before we left his place," Adam told her. "He wanted to check about Lindy. They admitted they got the family together and shared Bill's news about your safety and that you were going to be at your brother's house. They were all getting ready to drive to Nevada to collect you."

"They'll kill me with love," Chelsea said.

"And not know they were doing it," Adam added.

"What about Florida?" she asked.

"You'd be willing to run away with me? You'd be breaking several laws, you know. False ID, no passport."

"I shot a man yesterday and killed one today," she said quietly. The reality of killing a man had been settling over her heart like a shroud, growing heavier as the hours passed.

Adam covered her hand with his and squeezed it. "You didn't have a choice," he said.

She nodded. As bad as killing someone felt, sitting there lamenting a necessary act seemed self-indulgent, even selfish, especially as Adam had fired the shot that ended the siege and ultimately saved them all.

He pulled into a gas station a few minutes later and they topped off the tank, added two quarts of oil to the gluttonous engine and bought sandwiches in the attached deli. They mutually decided to eat while they kept driving.

The hours piled up as they headed south, skirting Vegas, the world reduced to a million stars and broad stretches of empty land where the moonlight illuminated it. Sometime later, Adam's voice shook Chelsea from a half-dreamlike state, where she'd been lazing on a rope swing located inside her brother's chicken coop. She blinked a few times to reenter reality.

"We're both exhausted," he said.

She couldn't argue that.

"There's a motel up ahead. Let's get a room—two if you want—and try to get some sleep."

"One room," she said emphatically. She was not going to sit alone in a dark locked room, not tonight.

"Sounds good."

The motel was one of those long chains of connected rooms fronted with a swimming pool. A few motley-looking palms rustled in the slight breeze. Truthfully, Chelsea didn't care what kind of motel it was as long as it wasn't green, had beds and didn't move.

They checked in, paid cash, parked in front of unit 101 and took their meager possessions inside the room. Chelsea slumped onto a chair, and Adam sprawled across the bed.

After a while, they took turns showering. Dressed in clean clothes, they crawled beneath blessedly white sheets. For a few minutes, images of the day flashed in Chelsea's head like photographs. When Adam cleared his throat, she turned in his direction.

"You didn't get the answers to any of your questions today like we planned," he said.

"I met my brother and his wife," she said. Speaking into the dark room without the benefit of seeing his expression actually made talking easier. "He didn't really know you, though."

"I warned you about that," Adam said. "So, ask me anything you want or I can just start at the beginning and tell you the absolute factual truth of everything I know about you and everything you know—*knew*—about me."

She considered his question for several seconds.

"You're willing to be honest and forthright without fear of how it may make me or yourself look?"

"Yes."

"Why now?"

"Because it's time. And because it looks as though you're stuck with me. I can't protect you if you're not close and yet when you're close, I almost get you killed. Seems to me like you deserve to know whatever you want. But on the other hand, I have to warn you there's enough…information for you to absorb that it might hit you like an overload. Doc told me that one reason you might have this amnesia is because there's a part of you that doesn't want to remember everything, that you may be protecting yourself from …pain."

"From what you know of my life, is that a possibility?" she asked after a moment spent thinking about this comment.

"Yes," he said softly. "And that's why I'm giving you the option of asking questions and learning what you want at whatever pace you're comfortable with."

She thought for a second. "We were lovers," she stated baldly.

"Yes."

"I knew it," she whispered. "I've always known it."

"You see—" he began, but she reached over and pressed her fingers against his lips.

"Not tonight," she said. "I want every detail, all at once. I want to know exactly who and what I am and what my past and future look like. But I killed a guy today and I almost died and that's a lot to assimilate. If we're driving to Florida, we're going to have a lot of time in that green van. Time to talk and think. I'd like to wait until tomorrow, Adam."

"Are you sure? I've been dragging my feet. Today underlined the stupidity of that. You can handle anything."

"Do you think so?" she asked softly.

The bed creaked as he turned on his side. She felt his face move close to hers. "I know so," he whispered. "You're an amazing woman, Chelsea Ann Pierce, whether you know it or not…you're special, unique."

"Those sound like words spoken by a man who cares about a woman," she whispered.

His lips brushed her forehead. "That's because they are," he said.

She willed him to find her mouth with his, and as his warm breath caressed her skin, her heartbeat tripled. "Prove it," she said, unable to resist the temptation that seethed between them like molten lava. Something had changed that day, some mountain had been topped, a river forded—something had given way under the pressure of their experiences and left them in this bed, facing each other on a more level playing field than ever.

His lips finally touched hers, his perpetually short beard pleasantly brisk against her skin. The kiss lit a firecracker, sparked an explosion that cascaded into more as his hands slipped up under her T-shirt to caress her breasts. Another firecracker heralded the removal of her T-shirt and then the pink thong, and as she freed him of his boxers, they were at last naked together, alone, vulnerable and suddenly so in tune with each other they began to merge into one being.

His erection was hot and throbbing in her hand. He

gently pushed her onto her back and started kissing and sucking every square inch of her from her mouth to her throat, down to her breasts, to her belly, where his hands stroked her skin. He kissed her a hundred times between navel and pelvic bone as though treasuring that most female part of her body. When he found the center of her desire, she all but jumped out of her skin. He slid inside of her with gentle urgency as they easily fell into an ageless rolling rhythm, mouths locked together, breathing labored, her hands digging into the wonderful flesh of his butt, wanting him closer, wanting to absorb him. The thought of him ever leaving her created a second of anxiety, but that disappeared as he worked his magic. When they climbed to a crescendo it felt as if the motel must have surely rocked on its foundation.

When it was over, it still wasn't over. Within a few moments, he'd started kissing her again, slowly this time, thoroughly, discovering places that sent her soaring just as she investigated the miracle of his body with her hands and mouth. His muscles delighted her fingertips, his earlobes were delectable. She felt she could kiss his eyelids and cheekbones forever, smooth his fine hair away from his forehead until time stopped, luxuriate in the delight of his head buried in her throat, his heartbeat so strong it traveled right through his skin into her body. She knew they had done all this before, she could tell—they weren't carnal strangers. In fact, Adam Parish was the only real person in the world to Chelsea—everyone else from Doc Fisher to the bad guys to her brother seemed to be actors who took their few moments on the stage and then shuffled off.

Adam was real. Adam was permanent.

Eventually, spent and replete, they fell asleep in each other's arms.

Chelsea awoke around midnight. Adam's breathing was deep and even, his relaxed, heavy arm warm across her stomach. She laid there awhile, content in a way she hadn't been in her short memory, unafraid, ready to face the truths tomorrow would bring.

The minutes on the illuminated bedside table continued to pass and instead of growing sleepier, she grew more and more awake. Finally, she carefully moved his arm aside and slid to the edge of the bed. The springs creaked as she got to her feet but Adam's breathing didn't change. She smiled as she crossed the room to the bathroom, flicked on the light, closed the door behind her and washed her face.

Leaving the door ajar so a little light would spill into the bedroom, she found her discarded underwear and put it back on. Next she searched the bag that functioned as her suitcase and the brush she'd bought at the pharmacy. She went back into the bathroom to work the tangles from her hair. When she grabbed a towel, she accidentally knocked the clothes Adam had left draped over the towel rack to the ground.

Leaning over to retrieve things, her attention was caught by a small gold foil card wrapped inside a wrinkled receipt. The receipt was from the last gas station they'd visited. The card was a little battered, as though it had been stuffed somewhere and folded more times than intended. Without pausing to consider whether or not she should read it, she did just that.

"'My beloved Steven,'" she whispered. "'I think I know the location of the cabin you described the night you asked me to marry you. My plan is to drop these roses in the nearby river as a way of letting you go. I don't want to do this but the reality is you're dead. I'll never stop loving you just as I wonder if I'll ever understand what really happened to you or why that man from the government asked me a million questions but wouldn't answer even one of mine. Sometimes it feels as though I'm grieving a shadow. Goodbye, my love. Rest in peace knowing I will move heaven and earth to make a wonderful life for our baby. Yours forever, Chelsea.'"

It was dated the day of the crash. On numb feet, she left the bathroom and moved like a wraith to the small desk. She picked up the courtesy pen and found the small notepad. She wrote "Goodbye, my love." Before she'd finished the sentence, she knew she'd written the note.

Of course she'd written the note. She'd been the woman on the chopper. She tore the paper from the pad and tore it into pieces.

Wait, where was this baby she mentioned? And who was Steven?

She walked back into the bathroom, flushed the shredded paper and turned sideways to run her hand over the small swelling in her belly that she had attributed to her body type. The baby was inside of her, growing.

That realization left her dizzy and she sat down on

the edge of the tub. Adam had asked her over and over again if she was bleeding anywhere, if she hurt. He'd cautioned her about lifting heavy things and tonight, when they made love, he'd caressed her abdomen with such tenderness she'd noticed it despite the burning passion racing through her veins.

He knew. He knew she was pregnant and he hadn't told her. That meant Doc probably knew, too, and that's why he'd asked those questions when he examined her. Maybe even her brother knew—everyone knew about her baby but her!

What had happened to Steven, the man she'd apparently adored? Was his death the reason she couldn't remember anything? Was she scared to face the pain that painted every word in the note she'd written?

And when had Adam really come into the picture? Had he and Steven both loved her, both wanted her? Was it possible Adam killed Steven to achieve his goal? Would a man really go that far to win an ordinary woman like her?

She picked the foil card from the floor and read it again.

Maybe he would. She'd imagined herself capable of stalking Adam—was it so far-fetched to think *he* might have been stalking *her*? Could he have killed Steven to get what he wanted? Was he some kind of psychopath? Was the baby she carried Steven's or had Adam and she—?

How could she know? Adam would tell her what he wanted her to believe. He'd been doing that from the start—he'd as much as admitted it.

She recoiled at the thought of thinking these things about him, unwilling to believe the man she'd just given heart and soul to an hour before, the man she'd felt she instinctively knew down to his core could actually be her nemesis instead of her savior.

And yet all along, she'd known she'd too readily accepted the world as he presented it. She'd attempted to fight the temptation to fit into the niche he created, but she hadn't fought hard enough.

She stood abruptly and grabbed his jeans, looking for his wallet and identification, suddenly wondering if his name was even Adam Parish. The wallet wasn't there and she recalled the way he tucked it away every night. She'd thought he was protecting it from invaders of some kind—was he really just protecting it from her?

Sneaking back into the room, she pulled on shoes, jeans and a sweater and visually gave the room a quick search. She didn't see the wallet but what did it matter? He'd bought a car using that ID, Doc Fisher had called him by that name—what would seeing it on a license mean at this point?

She closed her hand around the van keys on the desk and opened the outside door. For a second she stared back at the bed, at the slumbering man. A huge part of her wanted to wake him up and demand explanations.

But she knew he would tell her whatever he believed she wanted to hear and she also suspected she would convince herself to be satisfied with that—for a while at least. The only way this would ever be resolved was to regain her memory of Steven, the helicopter, the roses, the baby…Adam. This was something she was going to have to do herself.

Closing the motel room door was like stepping on her own heart. She wasn't sure where she was going, just that she had to get away.

Chapter Ten

For one blissful moment Adam felt totally at peace. He opened his eyes with anticipation, anxious to see Chelsea. It was a small room and she wasn't in it. Getting up, he pulled on the boxers that had wound up on the floor and walked to the bathroom, where he could now see the door was ajar.

Tapping on it, he called her name. "Chelsea? Are you all right? May I come in?"

There was no answer. Alarmed now that she might be sick or have fainted, he opened the door wide and stood there for a second looking at the empty room, taking in the fact his jeans and shirt had fallen from the towel rack, but nothing else seemed amiss.

He draped his clothes back on the towel rack, wondering why the fact they'd fallen alarmed him. He always took his wallet out of his pants at night, was determined to guard that damning picture of him and Chelsea in San Francisco. He trotted back into the room, opened the closet and took his wallet from the highest shelf, where he'd shoved it under a stack of extra bedding.

The wallet held the photo, just as it always did. Today

he would use that picture and the foil card she'd included with her flowers to help explain to her his true identity and what they had meant to each other—

The thought sent a shiver through his heart. Where was the card?

It wasn't in his wallet. He must have taken it out when he bought oil for the van—it was bulky and a pain in the neck to shove into the wallet's limited space. He would have stuffed it in his jeans pocket.

He almost ran back to the bathroom, but he knew with every step that the card wasn't there. Chelsea must have found it.

What would she think?

He pulled on his clothes then scanned the table for the van keys. When he didn't see them, he opened the motel door.

The parking spot in front of their room was empty.

Within minutes, he'd put on his shoes and jogged over to the tiny motel office. It was still too early for a long check-out line, though one couple, who were apparently settling their bill, took up most of the available interior floor space. As he waited outside for them to finish, his mind raced with questions—how was he ever going to find Chelsea? Without the van, he was stranded here and even if he had wheels, what direction would she have gone?

How had he managed to handle this so poorly? Dumb question—he knew how. He'd put her off and put her off, trusting that some inner well of latent feelings for him would keep her by his side until he could face telling her the truth.

She now knew she was pregnant and no doubt believed the father of her baby and the love of her life was dead. She knew that she'd been traveling to drop flowers in an act of farewell. How would she interpret Adam's presence in the scenario?

Bottom line, she was alone out there somewhere. Holton knew about her, knew she made the perfect bait.

The couple came out of the office and Adam went inside. A young man who hadn't been at the counter the day before greeted him. "Checking out?" he asked. He looked to be in his late teens, with a gold stud in his left nostril and a half-shaved head.

"Probably," Adam said. "Have you been in the office long?"

"A couple of hours," he said. "I'm covering for my mom. What room are you in?"

"One-oh-one. Listen, did you happen to see the van parked in front of the room take off a while ago?"

"Nope."

"Do you remember if it was there when you got here this morning?"

"Nope." He narrowed his eyes. "Why? What's wrong?"

"My girl and I...had a fight," Adam said after a pause.

"She took off?"

"Yeah."

"Bummer."

"Yeah. But the thing is the van is old and unreliable and I'm worried about her. Is there a place to rent a car around here?"

"Man, you'd have to go back to Vegas for that."

Adam shook his head. This was getting worse by the moment.

"Or I could sell you my bike," the kid said.

"Your bike? What bike?"

"That Honda out there," he said, gesturing to the right of the office. Adam followed his lead and saw a beat-up old red motorcycle chained to the Coke machine.

"Does it run?"

"Like a bat out of hell," the kid said. "It's loud and I won't kid you, it's got…issues, but it's a real ass-burner. It'll take you where you want to go."

"And you're willing to sell it?"

"Mom kind of gave me an ultimatum," he said. "You know how it is."

"How much?" Adam asked.

"Eight hundred."

"Assuming it runs, I'll give you five and you throw in a helmet," Adam countered.

"Six," the kid said, then reached behind him and produced a black helmet that he set in front of Adam.

Adam considered his options, then picked up the helmet. "Get my bill ready, I'll be right back."

ADAM STRAPPED ALL his gear on the back and took off. The kid hadn't been bluffing—the bike could move. As he neared the outskirts of the tiny hamlet, he found a set of highway mileage signs pointing in three directions. Right to Los Angeles, straight ahead to Phoenix and left to Santa Fe.

Phoenix was near his home, but why would Chelsea choose to go to Arizona? Santa Fe was in the direction they would have taken had they been together, traveling toward Florida, but again, would Chelsea charge off into the unknown under the circumstances? He doubted it. With her memory compromised, there were already too many unknowns in her life. That left Los Angeles, which, of course, also meant a highway that would eventually lead to the Bay Area and her parents and family.

He turned right.

The bike was as loud as advertised, too. Between the sun beating down, the vibration of the cycle and the unrelenting screech of the engine, all his senses were on overload. The wound in his side protested every bump. He kept his eyes peeled for an old green van either traveling on the road, broken down beside it or pulled into a car rest or parking lot. The miles droned on, the trip made longer by his determination to stop at every establishment he passed to ask the proprietors if they'd sold oil to anyone with a green van or seen anyone in trouble. He was flying blind and he knew it.

It would have helped to have some idea when she took off. The earliest it could have been was after they made love. That meant she could have up to a four-hour lead. Four hours at even fifty miles an hour gave her two hundred miles. She could be approaching Los Angeles by now if the car had held up. How in the world would he ever find her there? He'd have to head to the small town of Bodega Bay and her parents and hope to intercept her but that could be days from now. Judging by what had happened at Chelsea's brother's place,

Holton must have placed someone in Bodega Bay to watch her family and listen to her talkative sister. Was that someone still there?

The debacle at Bill's place also brought out the undeniable fact that the three men sent there to fake an accidental bombing had failed in their attempt and subsequently disappeared off the face of the earth. Whoever had sent them had to have figured this out by now.

And what about Ron Ballard? If a US marshal was involved in this, how much did he know and what kind of advantages did he have when it came to ferreting out information? Adam had bought two vehicles now using his real ID. Did someone have a flag out for that contingency? Adam didn't know, but he wouldn't be surprised to find that Ballard had a way of keeping abreast of Adam's location.

No matter. There was nothing to be done but continue trying. This was his lover and his baby—his family, his life and all of it was in danger because of him. There was no quitting.

AFTER FIFTY MILES, Adam admitted to himself that he needed a break of more than a couple of minutes. Coffee, maybe something to eat, a respite from constant vibrations and the pain to the knife gash that flared as he leaned forward to grasp the handlebars. He pulled up in front of a small gas station advertising cold drinks and snacks.

Inside, he found an older man behind the counter. He ordered coffee and snatched a prepackaged pastry off the shelf then downed one of his antibiotics and a couple of aspirin. A few other travelers meandered around. Probably, like Adam, they loitered as much for the air conditioning as they did the merchandise.

Adam spied a produce section in the cooler and chose an apple to take along for a future snack. As he approached the counter to pay for everything, a tinkling bell announced another man coming into the store through a small back door. He nodded at Adam as he walked behind the counter. "I finally got it out of her, Sam," he said to the guy ringing up Adam's purchases.

"Yeah? What's her problem, then?"

"She's broke. We're going to have to help her out."

Sam shook his head. "We can't just give her money," he said.

"The kid doesn't have a penny. Don't be so damn cheap."

"I'm frugal, not cheap," Sam said with a sigh as he handed Adam his change. He shook his gray head. "On the other hand, I guess we can't have her parked out back forever. What does she need exactly?"

"A couple of quarts of oil, that's all."

Adam looked up quickly.

"That's not too bad," said Sam. "Okay, just give it to her and get her out of here."

"Someone needs oil for their vehicle?" Adam said.

The second man nodded. "Some little gal. Needs a couple of quarts."

"Where is she?"

Sam's eyes narrowed. "Why do you want to know?"

Adam smiled. "I had some bad luck lately. Someone helped me get back on my feet on the condition I pay it forward. This sounds like an opportunity to do just that. Plus I'm a mechanic. If there's something else wrong with her car, maybe I can help."

Sam nodded, obviously delighted to get off the hook. "She's parked out back under the only tree around. Been sitting out there all morning."

"She was too shy to ask for a handout," the second guy added. "I had to worm what was wrong out of her. It doesn't seem she knows anything about cars and that old van she's driving is on its last legs."

"Point the way," Adam said, "but first sell me a half-dozen bottles of motor oil. Might as well get her a few spares. Oh, and add in one of those breakfast burritos you have back there, a cup of coffee and a bottle of orange juice."

"That's mighty decent of you," the second man said as he filled a box with the right number of oil bottles from a display. Sam gathered the food and rang everything up, a big smile on his wrinkled face as he presented the total to Adam.

CHELSEA, SITTING INSIDE the sliding side door of the wretched van and fanning herself with a folded road map of Montana, heard approaching footsteps and held her breath. It was no doubt Thomas, the nice older guy who worked at the store. He'd been out to talk to her three different times until she'd finally admitted she didn't have the money to pour more oil into this blasted engine.

If she hadn't bought that breakfast yesterday, she'd have had enough to pour oil into this thing at least until

California. But she knew that would have only been a stopgap measure. The Bay Area was a long way from Los Angeles. Gas, oil, food—all of it took money. She'd set off ill-prepared, fleeing on emotional energy alone, not factoring in logic.

Hopefully, Thomas had taken pity on her and was bringing the oil, as he'd hinted he might. It was either accept a handout or sit out here until she keeled over from heat exhaustion or, worse, Adam found her. Not good, not when she had a baby to consider.

The footsteps grew closer and she stood up, a smile in place for Thomas, a smile that slid from her lips when she saw Adam instead. She sat back down on the floor of the van and covered her eyes with her hands.

He sat down beside her. A moment later, she smelled the aroma of hot coffee. "You found me," she whispered through her fingers.

"Dumb luck," he said. "Here, I thought you might need this."

She dropped her hands. Ignoring the proffered coffee, she met his gaze. "I had to leave," she said.

"I know. You saw the card, didn't you? The one you wrote."

"Yes. I know about my baby, I know about Steven. Adam, who was he? Did you—did you kill him?"

He set aside the coffee and dug his wallet out of his pocket as he answered. "In a way, but not how you think," he said. He opened the wallet, took out a photograph and handed it to her.

She faced both of their images, standing side by side, smiling, Adam's arm around her shoulder. They both looked relaxed and happy. It was dated two months earlier. And there was her handwriting again. It identified Adam as Steven. "I don't understand—"

"You will in a while," he said. "I wish you'd woken me up and asked me about this," he added.

"I was scared and angry and didn't trust my feelings. After what we shared last night—"

"Wasn't that a pretty good reason to give me a chance to explain?" he interrupted.

"You've had days to explain," she said softly as she gave in to the aroma of fresh, hot coffee and picked up the paper cup.

"True. Okay, here we go. My name really is Adam Parish. I really did turn state's evidence against a snake of a man accused of human trafficking. I got him convicted. Because of his threats and connections, the US Marshals offered me a new identity in a new state and I took it. I moved to San Francisco, where I got a job working construction. I met you just as I said I did. I didn't tell you about my past because it wasn't allowed and because I knew it might put you in danger if you knew the truth. I fell in love with you and you with me. All that is true."

"And you're my baby's father?"

"Absolutely."

"How did you 'die?'"

"One of the snake's men found out where I was. I'm not sure how. He came after me, right on the night I asked you to be my wife. I managed to subdue him."

"You mean you killed him," she said.

"Yes. I had worked out my own escape route if this

event should ever come to pass. I'd purchased a plane and stored it out of town, kept my own identity… Anyway, there was this marshal who more or less 'handled' me and I didn't trust him. I knew if my cover was blown I'd have to disappear for good, so I staged my death by putting the plane on autopilot and parachuting to safety. The plane went down into a glacier lake. I knew they couldn't dredge it. The only body aboard the plane was that of the would-be killer."

"And you didn't tell me."

"I didn't know you were pregnant, Chelsea."

"But you knew I would mourn you, didn't you?"

"Yes."

"And you left me behind, anyway, ignorant and grieving. I can't imagine how devastated I was." He said nothing. "So the police questioned me. I gathered that much from the note."

"Yes, they apparently did."

"Who knows what I told them?"

"You didn't really know anything except what I told you," he said.

"The story of our relationship. You in control of all of the information, calling the shots. It seems the only independent thing I did was my ill-fated grand gesture to leave you at the motel."

"Chelsea—"

"One of the bad guys somehow got on that helicopter with me," she continued. "And he died when the chopper crashed and you were there on the scene because you weren't dead, you were hiding."

"Yes," he said, his body tense.

"So why didn't you explain all of this when you found me on the chopper?"

"I planned to, but then I discovered your memory was gone. I decided to wait until it…came back."

"You could have shown me that picture."

"By then I'd given you my real name instead of the Steven that's written on the photo."

"So in other words, you would have had to tell me you left me."

He nodded.

She stared into his eyes. "I can tell from that note that you broke my heart," she said, "and I have to assume since you didn't know I was coming to drop those flowers that you didn't even try to contact me. You just…left."

He winced but met her gaze. "That's pretty much it," he said. "I wasn't sure the hit man had come alone. I couldn't chance anyone following me to you, which they did, anyway. These people are dangerous. I loved you—love you—too much—"

She held up her hand to silence him. "Your decision caused an innocent pilot—at least he might have been innocent—to die, and you've lied or omitted things since the moment you laid eyes on me again. And now we're running for our lives and more people have been hurt or killed. So tell me this, Adam. When does it stop?"

"When we get to Florida."

"No. That won't stop it. They'll still look for you. And why? Revenge? In the face of all the mayhem and death, doesn't that reason seem kind of implausible? What else aren't you telling me?"

"I don't know," he said. "That's the truth. I've thought the same thing about the degree of vengeance but I have no idea why it's so intense."

"But you've kept with one plan. Escape. Run."

He looked stricken and any pleasure she might have found in challenging him to assuage her own hurt fled. She yearned to cup his face and kiss his lips, ached to hold him. She could tell he loved her, or at least thought he did, and she knew she had deep feelings for him, but those feelings were confused. The ultimate conclusion was that the reality he had created and was continuing to create had no future, especially in light of the fact there was an innocent new life to consider.

"From the beginning, my plan was to get out of the country and let all this animosity wear down. I've been a loner since my dad died. It's my default nature to take care of unpleasant things on my own and not involve anyone else."

"But you asked me to marry you. And whether you knew it or not, you helped create another life."

"I know. And since you came back into the picture, my focus has been to make sure you're safe. I haven't been very successful at that."

"Maybe it's time for a new plan," she said.

"Like what?"

"I don't know, like being part of a team that gets to the bottom of what's really going on, by letting me help you. By thinking of me as an adult to be leaned on and not a child to be protected. I would like my baby to have a father."

"You're willing to stick with me?"

"I don't know, Adam. Long-term, I can't promise anything. I don't know for sure how deep my resentment toward you runs and I might not know that until my memory returns. If Doc Fisher was right about my amnesia being caused by fear of pain, it's pretty obvious to me that you're the cause."

"I know," he said.

"However, I will stay with you as long as it takes for you to get your life back and assure a future, to make sure our baby won't fall victim to this same danger. That I'll stick around for."

"That's a beginning," he said.

She nodded.

They sat in silence for several minutes until he finally got to his feet. "I'll get the van running again and we'll take off."

"If you change your mind and run again, you're doing it alone," she warned him.

He touched the top of her shoulder and stared down at her. "You're right, it's time to get to the bottom of this."

"How?"

"By using my head instead of my feet. All I ask is that you trust me."

"I'll try," she said as she stood. "It's up to you."

He reached into the box containing several quarts of oil and took out a bottle of juice and a wrapped burrito, which he offered to her. "This will give you something to do while I get this heap running."

"Thanks."

He leaned toward her and she moved toward him. The kiss felt like a lover's version of a handshake at first, but then Adam gripped the back of her head and touched her lips with his tongue, and the kiss blossomed into more.

She pulled away. He stared into her eyes and she could see that he understood. They could not go back to where they'd been just hours before. She would stick by him for their baby's sake.

That's all she could guarantee.

Chapter Eleven

"We're going to Hard Rock, Arizona," Adam announced after he'd rigged a ramp to roll the motorcycle into the back of the van. He tied the bike upright and slammed the door. "We're going to need to change our appearances."

She climbed into the passenger seat as he got behind the wheel. "Is Hard Rock a big place?" she asked. "Do you know a lot of people?"

"It's pretty small, actually, and I hardly know anyone. I moved there from Tucson to take the job as bodyguard for Devin Holton and his wife, Aimee. Which brings up the matter that we have to assume Holton's men have reported my current bleached hair and your description must have been circulated. Have you ever wanted to be a redhead?"

"How do I know? But what the heck, why not? What do we do when we get to Hard Rock?" she asked.

"For starters, I want to get some idea what Holton's wife did after he went to prison."

"Wouldn't she just stay at their house?"

"It's a big estate. The government must have seized

it upon conviction. But there may still be someone I know hanging around up there, so I can't poke around as Adam Parish. I think I'll use my dad's name, Frank, and my mother's surname, Mason. As for what comes after that, it depends on what I find. Holton had a few cronies—maybe I can infiltrate them and get wind of what's going on."

"Sooner or later, won't they recognize you?"

"Maybe not. A good bodyguard's face is almost invisible. You're more a walking muscle with a gun than you are a human being."

"But they must have seen you at the trial."

"Most of them stayed away from that trial unless they were subpoenaed. It had been moved to Tucson so it wasn't in their backyard. Plus I grew a big old beard and wore a ponytail."

"I'll need a new name, too," she said. "I think I'll call myself Daisy Hanks."

"Cute," he said. "Let's get another room and change our appearance."

Two hours later, Chelsea had short red hair and bright red lips. Adam's hair was the same length as his beard, less than half an inch. When he donned the reflective glasses Chelsea had chosen, he hardly recognized himself.

Adam admitted that he dreaded the moment Whip learned he was back in Arizona. The man had made it pretty clear that he was in favor of Adam getting out of the country—this change of plans would no doubt alarm him.

On the other hand, maybe he'd heard something

about US Marshal Ron Ballard or discovered whoever was acting as liaison between Holton and the outside. Or even better, maybe he'd gleaned some clue as to why Holton seemed to be moving heaven and earth to hunt down and eliminate Adam.

IT TOOK UNTIL the next afternoon to get to Hard Rock and by the time they drove into the small hamlet, they were tired, hot and hungry. They stopped to eat tacos from a food truck doing brisk business and settled at one of several picnic tables, commenting on how good the food was with every other bite. Chelsea wasn't fooled by Adam's idle chatter. His obvious case of nerves set her on edge.

The feeling was enhanced when he suddenly shaded his face with one hand and looked down at the table. "What's wrong?" she asked.

"Dennis is over there."

"Who's Dennis?"

"Dennis Woods, a very old friend. He's the one who bought my parents' house when I went into the program."

She looked toward the food truck. Two women ordered lunch at the window, while one man stood behind them, hands shoved in his pockets. He caught Chelsea staring at him and flashed her a brilliant smile. She looked away at once.

"Did he see you?"

"Yes. But remember, he doesn't know me from a hole in the wall. He probably thinks I'm flirting with him."

"We'd better get out of here," he said.

But Dennis turned as Adam stood. His eyes narrowed and then he grinned. "Adam?" he called. "Adam Parish, is that you? Man, I haven't seen you in forever. Where the hell have you been?"

He said all this as he strode across the grass, headed for Adam, who was powerless to quiet him without creating more of a scene.

"Dennis," Adam said, extending his hand.

Dennis shook it vigorously, then turned his attention to Chelsea. "Do we have you to blame for Adam's mysterious disappearance? Not that I would blame him."

Adam performed the introductions. "What are you doing all the way up here in Hard Rock?" he asked.

Dennis laughed. "It's only an hour or so from Tucson, you idiot. Anyway, I'm doing a job, what else? My company is replumbing the old Stop and Shop. They're making it into a tropical fish store." He paused for a second. "Tell me what you've been up to. I called around trying to find you—"

"Why? Is anything wrong?"

Dennis laughed. "Man, you're jumpy, aren't you?" He looked at Chelsea and shook his head. "Our boy is wound a little tight."

"Tell me about it," she said with a smile for Adam.

Dennis slapped Adam on the shoulder. "Well, the main reason was to tell you that Stacy is pregnant again. As a matter of fact, the baby is due in three weeks. We're growing right out of your old house."

"Congratulations," Adam said after a swift glance at Chelsea's stomach.

"The other reason is the exterminators found something that must belong to you when they were crawling around the basement looking for termites."

"What do you mean?"

"A sealed box, pushed way up in the crawl space under the smallest bedroom there in the front. Someone wrote Do Not Open on it. Ring any bells?"

"None."

"Didn't your dad build that house when you were a baby?"

"Yeah."

"So the box has to have belonged to someone in your family, ergo, as the last surviving member, it's yours."

"So what's in it? Discarded toys, old dishes?" Adam asked.

"I asked around but no one knew where you'd gone, so I opened it to make sure it wasn't trash or something. It looked like a lot of papers so I taped it back up. It's heavy, I will say that."

"Interesting," Adam said in an offhand manner. But Chelsea heard the curiosity in his voice and she suspected Dennis did, too. "Where is it now?" he added.

"We were getting ready to paint the inside of the house so I took it and a lot of other things to our storage garage," Dennis said. "Good thing I did, too, because the house was broken into a few days later."

"Oh, no, did you lose a lot?"

"Just some electronics, stuff like that, but they tore the place up pretty good. Thankfully no one was home, no one got hurt." He paused and shook his head. "Sorry, bro, I forgot for a moment about your mom and...everything."

"It's okay."

Dennis looked at Chelsea. "His mom was the greatest. Always went to bat for 'her kids.' Remember, Adam, remember that girl who ran away from home?"

"I remember," Adam said, his voice subdued.

"Your mom was determined to find her and get her back in school. Ms. Parish was just outright amazing."

"I wish I could have known her," Chelsea said.

"Yeah." He looked back at Adam. "I'm real glad you're back. I hope you can stick around."

"Me, too," Adam said.

"I know Stacy will want to see you. And you, too," he added with a glance at Chelsea. "Maybe you guys could come for dinner."

"Let's talk about it in a few days," Adam said. "Right now would it be too much trouble for you to get the box out of storage?"

"No trouble at all. The place is on the way home. I'll be back in Hard Rock tomorrow so I could give it to you then. Will you still be here?"

"I'll be here."

"Say four or so, right where we're standing?"

"Sounds good. And until we can talk some more, mind not saying anything to anybody about my being here?"

"Always the man of mystery," Dennis said. "Sure, why not?" He glanced back at the taco truck. "I'd better go order something. See you tomorrow." He looked at Chelsea and added, "Great meeting you."

As Dennis returned to the truck, Adam and Chelsea walked across the street to the van.

"You okay?" she asked him as he unlocked and opened the back door. He sat on the floor of the van and pulled her to stand between his legs before wrapping his arms around her waist and resting his head against her breasts.

"Adam?" she prodded. "Are you okay? Do you have any idea what's inside that box?"

"No," he said, lifting his head to look at her. "It's hard to picture my mother crawling around under the house with all the spiders and bugs, so that leaves Dad. I can't stop thinking about that appointment my mom had with the police chief. Dad could have cleaned out any evidence she'd intended to give the chief to prove he was running wild. Maybe he had a diary or something, maybe he crossed a legal or ethical line—maybe he hid what he found under the house after he—"

"Killed her? Oh, Adam, honey, you're borrowing trouble," Chelsea cautioned. "Wait and see what's in the box."

"I've never told anyone this," he whispered without looking at her. "I heard the fight they had the night before she was killed. She was begging him to tell the chief something and he kept saying he couldn't. He was drinking, she was crying. The last thing I heard was her saying she'd do it herself and then it sounded like he slapped her. I left the house when he started apologizing."

"Adam, listen to me," Chelsea said, lifting his chin to stare into his deep gray eyes. "You were a kid interpreting what you heard. Who knows what was really going on or who slapped who?"

He rested his head against her again, hugging her tight as though grounding himself. "It killed me not to tell Dennis you're having our baby."

"Why didn't you?"

"That's what normal people do. They hold normal conversations. I don't feel very normal right now, do you?"

"No."

He was quiet. She'd been trying to stay at least a little aloof, but his vulnerability shook her. She smoothed the back of his head and ran her hands down his neck to his broad shoulders. "Being here is hard for you, isn't it?"

"I just hadn't counted on running into Dennis and all these old feelings… He lived three doors down from me when we were in school. I've known him forever, but so much has happened in the last year or so that today he seemed like a stranger." He looked up at her, the expression in his gray eyes unfathomable.

"When this is over, we'll go have dinner with him and Stacy, who I assume is his wife. You'll have a couple of beers and talk about old times—it will all come back." She leaned down and brushed his lips with hers.

"How do you know?" he murmured.

"Isn't this what you keep telling me? My memory will return and presto, I'll have a family I remember, friends, a career…our past?"

"For better or worse," he said.

"Exactly."

He stood up. "Then it's time to make it happen. I'm going to take the motorcycle up to the Holton place."

"Okay. I'll take the van into the city center. I need

some walking-around money." He gave her his wallet. "Whoa," she said as she glimpsed a row of large-denomination bills.

"You're looking at the bank of Adam," he said.

"What about later, when this is over?"

"I'll have to make more," he said. "But right now, my main goal is to keep both of us alive." As she stared at the money and absorbed his words, he took out a fifty and handed it to her. "Is that enough?"

"Plenty. Adam, did you ever tell me what kind of human trafficker Holton was?" she asked as he opened the back of the van and climbed inside. Kneeling by the bike, he started untying the knots he'd created to keep it upright.

"The worst kind. Young girls used as sex slaves. While hiding behind a more or less legitimate commodities business, he coerced, corrupted, bought and sold teenagers."

Chelsea shuddered. "That's just awful."

"Yes. And now he's sitting in a nice clean jail cell getting three meals a day and orchestrating this assault on you and me and heaven knows who else, while many of the girls whose childhoods he stole still struggle to survive drug addictions and sex slavery. Doesn't seem very fair, does it?"

Chelsea helped him get the bike out of the van. "That's an understatement but at least you helped put an end to it. That's got to make you feel good."

He grabbed the helmet. "It does. I couldn't save those who were lost into the ether but at least it's not still continuing, at least not with Holton."

She stared into his eyes, caught up in a wellspring of emotion. Chills ran up her spine and arms, radiating across her shoulders, and in a complete turnaround, she suddenly wished they were on their way to Florida, still running, still hiding.

Instead they stood in what felt like the lion's den.

THIRTY-EIGHT MILES of more or less straight highway bordered by fields, cactus, rocks and tired old buildings connected Hard Rock and the Holton property. Hazy mountains in the distance glimmered in the afternoon heat. Many of the small farms and ranches along the way could only be reached via long, dusty driveways, leaving acreage close to the highway. One farm appeared to have tried raising a grain crop. Whatever it had been, it was now a few acres of what looked like shriveling yellow weeds. In another month, even those would dry up and disappear.

Adam wasn't sure the mesa that Holton had owned was really a mesa. It did have three sheer, vertical sides, but one sloped enough for some enterprising soul in the past to have created an access road. This road was usually traffic-free, so Adam was surprised to pass a couple of trucks. He wondered if there were new owners now.

The small guard shack at the top of the road stood empty and he drove onto the property unchallenged. He knew from experience that the main house was at the far northern edge. Other than the main house and the staff quarters, the only other major structures on the property were a new storage shed and an old house and goat barn that had been occupied years before by homesteaders, who'd tried to raise goats but gave up after several disasters wiped out the herd.

He slowed down the bike when he caught sight of a building under construction. He came across what appeared to be a road leading in that direction and, out of curiosity, he turned.

Judging from the boxlike contours, it was going to be a modern-looking structure. Had the acreage been divided into lots and sold? Would the mesa someday resemble a subdivision? That would really set Holton off. He'd liked being the king of his mesa.

Half a dozen vehicles cluttered the work site, along with more than a dozen workmen. Adam stopped the motorcycle next to a white trailer marked with a sign that identified it as the project office for Diaz Construction. The familiar noises of saws, hammers, drills and men shouting to be heard over the din filled his ears and reminded him of San Francisco.

This was as good a place as any to start asking questions and narrowing down possibilities. No doubt these people would also know what had become of Aimee Holton. He took off his helmet but kept the sunglasses in place. Who knew whom he might run in to around here? He wasn't taking any chances of being recognized.

CHELSEA FOUND A parking spot and took off on foot. Her plan was to strike up a conversation with someone willing to talk about Aimee Holton. In a small town, Devin Holton's arrest, trial and conviction had to have fueled the rumor mill for months. Surely someone would know where his wife went after she lost her home.

Occasionally Chelsea caught an unexpected glimpse of the small bump in her abdomen in a shop window. Until today, she'd not yet started to think of herself as a mother-to-be and that realization now filled her with a mix of joy and trepidation. What if her memory never came back? Sure, she could get reacquainted with her old life, with family and friends, but would she ever regain the connection to them she must have once felt? On top of that, the possibility of losing Adam terrified her, but that created another conundrum. Did she feel so close to him because he was the only familiar person on earth? She'd accused him of fear—was she just as guilty?

Well, at least she and her baby would start out on the same playing field.

The first business she reached was a furniture store. The sole saleswoman was so focused on selling the brocaded chair Chelsea had feigned an interest in that all her leading questions and comments fizzled out and died.

Next she found a clothing store, and for a moment, she stood outside the window admiring the pink, form-fitting dress on the mannequin, as it was so unlike the jeans and T-shirts she currently lived in. She wondered for a second what her closet at home looked like, then stepped inside. The dress from the window seemed to call to her from the back of the store, where one just like it shone as a glittery beacon of femininity. She wove her way through the circular racks and this time was able to touch the silky fabric and admire the daring plunge of the neckline. She could almost imagine Adam's expression if she showed up wearing this dress...

"Beautiful, isn't it?" a saleswoman said, startling Chelsea out of her daydream.

"Very."

"It would be lovely on you." She looked Chelsea up and down, and took another off the rack. "I bet this is your size."

"I couldn't," Chelsea said.

The saleswoman smiled. "It's a slow day and I would love to see this dress on a grown woman who can pull it off. Please?"

Her comment seemed strange to Chelsea. She shrugged. "Why not?"

After putting it on, she stared at her red-headed bedazzled reflection in the mirror. She had a gut feeling she'd never dressed like this in her life, but she had to admit the garment made her breasts look bountiful and her hips enticing. She opened the curtain and faced the saleswoman, a striking brunette, who smiled.

"That dress was made for you."

"I'm pregnant," Chelsea said. It was the first time she'd said it to anyone but Adam.

"That's wonderful. I guess you won't need a tight-fitting slinky dress, will you?"

"Not really," Chelsea agreed. "But it was fun to try it on. I wondered, though, why you said what you did, you know, about seeing the dress on a grown woman?"

The saleswoman straightened the skirt. "Someone else bought this same dress this morning. Actually, it was an older guy buying it for his granddaughter. She couldn't have been over fifteen and she appeared mortified by the way she looked in it. I tried to talk the man out of buying it but he said she'd like it when she got used to it."

"It really bothered you," Chelsea commented.

The woman nodded. "The look on the kid's face got to me. Grandfathers shouldn't shop for young girls."

"Isn't it hard on guys of all ages to figure out women's attire?" Chelsea asked softly.

The woman shook her head. "Maybe, but anyone could see the child was way too self-conscious to wear something so revealing. It'll make her want to hide in a corner." She caught herself and sighed. "I have a thirteen-year-old daughter at home. I guess I'm kind of sensitive to things like this. Now, what are you looking for?"

Chelsea started to make up a story about needing a yellow blouse and then decided against inventing a story. "Do you know Aimee Holton?"

"Kind of," the woman said. "She came in here once, scoffed at our selection and left." Her expressive eyebrows furrowed. "Why do you ask?"

"I was wondering what she's like," Chelsea said, and suddenly did a one-eighty and invented a tale to explain her curiosity. "I'm a chef and I'm thinking of working for her."

"Yeah, I heard her cook quit again."

"Really?"

The chime on the door rang as a woman entered the store. *"Buenas tardes,"* the saleswoman called. *"Ahora vuelvo."*

The customer waved a hand. *"Bien."*

And Chelsea almost gaped. She'd understood every word! Who knew?

"Ms. Holton has an ad up at the culinary store across the street and the girls over there like to…chat," the saleswoman said, turning her attention back to Chelsea. "They told me she wanted them to cater a party she has planned for two days from now but they declined." She arched her eyebrows. "You can extrapolate from that what you like."

Chelsea nodded. Once outside she spied the culinary store across the street and crossed the road. If anyone knew about Aimee Holton, it sounded like it would be the people who ran this store.

Chapter Twelve

Adam hadn't taken three steps before the trailer door opened and a slender middle-aged guy carrying a set of blueprints emerged. He descended the two stairs before addressing Adam. "You must be here about the electrician job," he said. "You have to talk to that man walking up the path."

Adam turned toward the path leading up from the new construction site. He found a man with piercing black eyes and colorful tattoos running up his tanned arms. The hard hat perched on his black hair was emblazoned with Diaz Construction on its brim. "I'm not here about a job," Adam said. "I used to know a family who lived up here."

The man with the blueprints shook his head. "I'm a recent transplant from New Mexico," he said. "The only name I know is Holton."

The other man approached and introduced himself. "Diego Diaz," he said. "The people who originally built the little farm on the other side of this property were named Mendoza."

Adam introduced himself as Frank Mason. "I must

have the wrong place." He raised his gaze to peer over the few trees and contour of the land. "Looks like the house you're building is a big one."

"Sixty-five hundred square feet," Diaz said. He looked at the man with the blueprints. "You headed back to town?"

"Yeah. I'll work on the modifications and get back to you by Monday."

"Thanks."

"Owners change their mind?" Adam asked Diaz.

"Don't they always?"

"Every job I've ever worked on, yeah, they sure do."

"You've worked construction? Are you here about the electrician job?"

"When I got tired of being a cop I worked for a crew up north. But, you know, electricity is a different matter than pounding nails or putting up drywall."

"That it is. You from around here?"

"Just traveling through. On vacation, kind of."

"That must be nice."

Adam laughed. "I'm on a shoestring so that means not quite as nice as you might think. I stop here and there and work for a few days, then move on."

Diaz groaned. "Sounds kind of cool. At home I've got a pregnant wife and two little kids and out here I have a finicky owner who changes her mind every other day. Now she wants a designer refrigerator that's going to take up two thirds of the wall which means the stove has to be moved and rewired. Last week it was a sky-light in the entry. — It's one thing after another with

Aimee. Anyway, what you're doing right now sounds pretty good sometimes."

Aimee still lived here? How could that be? As Adam commiserated with Diaz, he noticed Diaz studying him. "So, tell me, Frank," he said at last. "How would you feel about a short-term job? I'm asking because you said you used to be a cop and this might be right up your alley."

"What do you have in mind?" Adam asked.

"A sort of watchman thing."

"Are you losing supplies or something?"

"We take our tools with us every night or lock them up in the trailer, but someone is messing with stuff and now it's escalated to vandalism. They've been spray-painting some pretty nasty words, too. I mean, given the nature of what landed Mr. Holton in prison, it isn't too surprising, but that's not his wife's fault. We clean it up when we find it so she won't see it. That takes time and as they say, time is money. I think it's a few teens from town, but I need to know for sure before I go accusing them. They're well-off kids, the sheriff would laugh at me if I came to him with nothing but suspicions."

"Why not just put someone at the guard shack?"

"The owner nixed a guard on the road. I'd stay out here myself, but the wife needs me at home and my guys won't do any overtime until the boss catches up on their wages. Anyway, there's a room off the work-shop you could bunk in. It's not fancy—"

"Neither are the motels I frequent," Adam interjected.

"You'd make my life easier, earn a little cash, then ride off into the sunset just like the Lone Ranger."

Adam laughed, but then grew serious. "I'm not interested in getting involved with the law," he said. "If your proof requires eyewitness testimony, I'll have to pass."

"Then get some kind of proof that doesn't depend on your input."

"Like what?"

"Listen, you're a big guy with a certain...air about you. I have faith you'll figure something out."

Adam stuck out his hand. "I'll give it a shot. If I think it's impossible, I'll let you know so you can hire someone else."

"Deal. Come on down to the house and I'll fill you in."

After an enlightening hour, Adam pulled on his helmet and mounted his bike. He had a job, but he also had misgivings. In his desire to look different to Holton's henchmen, he'd actually gone back to looking more like himself, as proven by Dennis's easy recognition of him. Aimee might do the same—they had lived on top of each other for the six months he worked for and spied on her husband. His hope was that from the outside like this, on her land but not in her space, he could watch who came and went.

There was only one hitch. Nights spent here meant nights alone for Chelsea. How would that work? If the danger was here, how could he leave her?

The road curved to the right and straightened out as it approached the exit. His mouth all but dropped open when he saw an unmistakable green van drive through the gate. What was Chelsea doing here? Had something gone wrong in town? He automatically slowed down and pulled to the side of the road, assuming she would do the same, but she drove right past him, a slight nod of her head the only clue she'd registered his presence. He turned and watched her continue up the hill, fighting the urge to follow her.

Back in town, he parked on the street near the taco truck, found a palm tree casting a bit of shade and sat on the ground to wait.

CHELSEA FOUND A spot across the street from Adam's motorcycle. He sat on the ground several yards away but as he saw her park, he got to his feet and jogged across the street.

"What were you doing up on the mesa?" he asked before the door had even closed. "Why didn't you pull over and talk to me?"

She shook her head. He looked hot and stressed. "Man, your friend Dennis is right, you are wired. Remember the whole treat-me-like-an-adult speech I gave you yesterday?"

He sat very still for a moment and then took a deep breath. "I remember it. I'm sorry."

She smiled. "Thank you. I didn't stop because who knows who was watching that road and why advertise we know each other?" She shifted her body position so she could face him and added, "I went for a job interview."

"A job interview for what?"

"I'm the new cook. And the first thing Aimee Holton confided was that she is off to visit her husband a week from now."

"Looks like she's sticking by her man," Adam said. "Did she mention any reason she was off to see Devin?"

"She said she was 'reporting in.' She didn't explain what that meant."

"Interesting," Adam said. "Why exactly do you want a job working for her?"

"Isn't it obvious?" Chelsea asked. "I'll be inside the house. I can find out if she's bitter against you. I can see what makes her tick."

"Honey," he said, "I was her bodyguard for six months. Money makes her tick. Period."

"But you haven't seen her recently," Chelsea pointed out.

"True. The last time I saw her was when she sashayed into her husband's trial wearing several thousands of dollars' worth of designer clothes and claimed her husband was as innocent as the day was long. She called him a pillar of the community and a loving spouse while she dabbed at crocodile tears with a tissue. The jury saw right through her. It only took them two hours to reach a guilty verdict."

Chelsea smiled. "She may have changed. For instance, I have a feeling she has a new boyfriend."

"What gave you that impression?"

"She took a call while I was whipping her up a sandwich. It was clear she was talking to a man. She got all flirty. I think she mentioned the name Tom."

"Tom Nolan?"

"I didn't hear a last name. Who is Tom Nolan?"

"One of her hubby's cohorts. The prosecutor thought he might be involved in some of Holton's other criminal activities, but there wasn't enough evidence to indict him. The dude is married, though. Tell me how this job for Aimee Holton came about."

She explained about the women at the kitchen store not wanting to cater her party.

"I wonder if we could get a guest list," Adam mused.

"I could try," she said.

"Okay. Wait a second. Didn't Aimee ask to see some sort of identification?

"Nope. I mentioned my purse had been stolen and she shrugged. Said she paid the help in cash, so what did it matter? I don't think she's too worried about breaking little laws."

"Or maybe big ones, either," he said.

"Okay," Chelsea announced. "It's your turn. Tell me about your afternoon."

"Well, believe it or not, I got a job up there, too, kind of undercover work for the foreman building the new house. The job does come with a condition, however."

Chelsea raised her eyebrows. "You have to sleep with the boss? She's really quite attractive, but—"

"*My* boss is a forty-year-old dude with two kids and another on the way," he interrupted.

She grinned. "Good luck with that."

"The thing is I'm going to have to spend nights on the estate. Since I have to be away, maybe you could stay with Whip."

"I don't even know him! Besides, when Ms. Holton found out I was just traveling through town she got worried I wouldn't have a kitchen to practice making goodies. She offered me a room for a couple of days and I, of course, accepted."

"That means our deadline is Friday night. If we can't

figure out if anyone attached to the estate is involved in Holton's vendetta by then it's time to look elsewhere."

"Like where?"

"One problem at a time, okay?" He touched her face, ran a finger over her mouth. "You know, we'll both be up on that mesa tonight. Maybe we should arrange a midnight tryst."

She looked down at her hands.

He tilted her chin up and kissed her. She made sure to stay present in her head and not yield to his lips, but not because of him—her own motives and emotions were the ones she didn't trust.

"My love," he said against her cheek, his fingers brushing her ear before he lowered his head to kiss her again. It was clear he didn't have the same reservations about embracing intimacy that she did. However, he wasn't the one who'd been abandoned, the one subsequently misled. She didn't need her memory back to know how all of this had hurt.

He held her for a minute or more, his arms strong, his embrace sure, and despite her resolve, she was whisked back to the night they'd made love and how right it had felt, how familiar and exciting.

"This place is turning out to be Hard Rock's damn watering hole," he said into her ear.

The comment jarred her and she straightened up. "What?"

"The taco truck. That's Whip walking across the grass. What in the world is he doing here?"

"Let's go find out," Chelsea said as she turned to get

a look at Adam's mentor. She saw a man in his fifties with gleaming gray hair, a tanned face and a beige suit.

She turned back to Adam. "I want to meet him."

"Might as well get it over with," Adam said and they both scooted out the passenger door and crossed the street. "He doesn't know I'm in Arizona," Adam explained as they stepped up on the opposite curb. "He's likely to be a little short with me."

"Why?"

"He thinks it's dangerous for me to be here."

Chelsea cast him a wry smile. "Well, isn't it?"

Adam smiled. "Yeah, I guess so. Especially if everyone I know shows up at this taco truck."

As if his policeman's instincts warned him of their approach, Whip turned. His expression went from curiosity to surprise as he saw them. He immediately broke away from the line and approached Adam, hand outstretched.

"Adam?" he said, as though not believing his eyes. "What are you doing here? I figure you had to get to Bill Pierce's place the day before yesterday. Good grief, do you have any idea how worried I've been?"

Adam performed introductions before responding to Whip's concerns. "We were ambushed," he said in a low voice. "The killers seemed determined to try to make it look like some giant survivalist explosive mishap or something. It wasn't well thought out and it didn't work."

"Was anybody hurt?" Whip asked.

"Bill's wife was injured but only the killers suffered casualties."

"Stupid bastards," he said. "But I haven't read or heard a thing about it."

"And you won't," Adam said, his voice ominous. He looked Whip over and added, "How are you? Why aren't you in uniform?"

"I have an interview this afternoon over in one of those buildings," Whip said, gesturing behind them. He dropped his voice again. "I thought you'd be in Florida by now. The thought of you just disappearing into thin air bothered me, but I have to admit not as much as seeing you standing out here in the open after what's gone down. What are you thinking?"

"We're on our way to Florida," Adam said. "I just wanted to show Chelsea Arizona before we left."

This was news to Chelsea.

Whip shook his head. "You're as reckless as your father was."

Adam seemed to ignore the remark. "Did you learn anything about Ron Ballard?"

"The marshal? A little. Rumor has it he's not a happy camper at his job. One of those disgruntled types, you know. In my book, that makes him dangerous. But worse, my contact said the man disappeared from California a week ago."

"Damn."

"Since you mentioned him, I've been thinking. Ballard has access to where you came from, who your friends are, everything. If he's the one after you, he'll look here next. He also has to know of any number of hired killers willing to make a few bucks by eliminating you—and yours. You opened a can of worms when you left the program."

"They failed to protect me," Adam insisted, his voice wary. "So I protected myself."

"At great cost," Whip said with a sidelong glance at Chelsea.

Adam looked down at the ground then into Chelsea's eyes. "You think I don't know that?" he muttered. She caught his hand and squeezed it tight. "Anyway, Ballard has no personal vendetta against me. The most he did was finger me and fail to warn me when trouble came. I can't see why he would come after me."

"You're being shortsighted. If he's guilty of fingering you and it comes out he's in danger of losing his job, you, son, constitute a loose end and men like Ballard don't like loose ends."

The silence stretched on and Whip shook his head. "Look, I know I'm being blunt. I'm just worried."

"Yeah," Adam said.

Chelsea attempted to break the tension with an off-topic remark. "We heard Aimee Holton is still living on the mesa."

Whip's eyebrows furrowed. "Aimee Holton? Why are you asking about her?"

"Everything Holton is on our radar right now," Adam said. "I thought the government confiscated his possessions after his conviction."

"All I know," Whip said, "is that Aimee's father is some wheeler-dealer back east. Tons of money. Bought the place through a holding company or something. The mesa didn't belong to Holton so the Feds couldn't touch it. For all intents and purposes, it's Aimee's. You did her a favor by helping to cut her loose from her husband." He clasped Adam's shoulder and softened his voice. "It's time to cut your losses. Does anybody else know you're here?"

"Just an old friend," Adam said.

"Old friends mention things to people and then they mention it to other people—"

"One way or another," Adam interrupted, "I've got to put an end to this."

Whip finally looked resigned to Adam's will. "Okay, if you won't listen to me, then at least let me help."

"I think it's better if you don't," Adam said. "Frankly, Whip, I want you out of this mess."

"I'm not the kind of guy to back down, you know that," Whip grumbled.

"Please."

He glanced at Chelsea again. "I really wish you two had stayed away from this place. I have a bad feeling—okay, but remember I'll be here if you need backup. You can always depend on me. All I want is your safety."

"I know. Thanks," Adam said. He took Chelsea's hand. "We'd better get going."

They took a few steps toward the van before Chelsea asked a question. "Why did you tell him you were here to show me Arizona? Don't you trust him?"

"With my life. But as you can see, he's overprotective at times. I gave in and owned up to my real reasons because he saw through me. He always does." He peered down into her eyes. "I'm banking the answers we need are up on that mesa."

She sighed. "Well, there's only one way to find out."

Chapter Thirteen

A youngish woman with a black ponytail opened the Holton door. With a sweep of her arm, she ushered Chelsea into the house.

"I'm Daisy Hanks, the new cook," Chelsea explained. "Ms. Holton is expecting me."

"Maria," the woman said, tapping her chest. *"Sigueme,"* she added as she gestured for Chelsea to follow her. Instead of going down the hall that appeared to lead to the bedroom wing of the spacious house, they went in the other direction, through the kitchen, where a teenage girl stood at the sink with her back to the room. Her jeans and T-shirt were good quality but hung on her small frame.

"Aqui," Maria coached, and led Chelsea past the laundry room and a small bath, ending in a square room with one window set high in the wall. "You sleep," the woman said in broken English. She pointed at the bed.

Chelsea assumed she didn't mean they had an early curfew but that this was Chelsea's room.

"It's very nice," Chelsea said.

A honking car startled both women. It sounded like it came from right outside the window.

"Mi amiga," Maria said with a smile. She nodded at Chelsea and hurried from the room.

"It was very nice to meet you," Chelsea called after her as Maria disappeared toward the kitchen. A minute later, Chelsea heard a nearby door close. She moved to the window and stood on tiptoe to look outside in time to witness Maria getting into a sedan driven by a friendly-looking woman. The car drove away almost at once.

It took Chelsea less than five minutes to unpack her bag and stow her toiletries in the bathroom. She returned to her room, sat on the edge of the bed and found herself missing Adam.

Time to put her mind elsewhere. Time to spy.

She returned to the kitchen, hoping she might run into Aimee. Snooping might be the reason she'd taken the job, but cooking was what was going to keep her around long enough to ferret something out.

The dark-haired teen still stood at the sink washing what Chelsea now saw was a cupboard's worth of stemmed glasses. "Hi," Chelsea said.

The girl turned anxious brown eyes in her direction. Only the bruise on her cheek distracted from the beauty of her heavily lashed eyes and smooth olive skin.

"How about I dry these for you?" Chelsea asked.

The teenager's expression remained blank. Chelsea opened a drawer and pulled out a clean cloth. She dangled it from her fingers in what had to be the universal language for "I can dry." Eyes now wide, the girl turned back to the sink.

Chelsea looked around to make sure they were alone.

Touching the girl's shoulder to get her attention again, she parroted Maria's gesture and touched her own chest. "*Yo me llamo* Daisy," she whispered in her newfound second language. It was the first Spanish she'd spoken in the house and the reason was probably silly. Aimee had made a point of asking Chelsea if she spoke Spanish. Something about the way she asked the question caused Chelsea to shake her head.

Was that James Bond-like or what?

For several seconds the girl said nothing but finally her lips parted. "Mariana."

"Mariana," Chelsea repeated. She touched her own cheek and added in Spanish, "Did someone hit you, Mariana?"

The girl's sudsy hand flew to her face. They stared at each other for a long moment, and then Mariana nodded.

"Who?" Chelsea asked in English. *"Quien?"*

Mariana's lips parted, then she quickly turned her head and went back to work right as Aimee Holton wafted into the room.

"You'd be wasting your time with that one even if she did speak English," Aimee said. "The girl has a foul temper."

"Don't you find it hard to communicate your wishes?" Chelsea asked. There was no way she was going to address the temper remark. For one thing, did that mean Aimee had inflicted that bruise on Mariana's cheek? And for another, the kid looked scared, not angry.

Aimee responded to that question by firing off a

flood of Spanish directed at Mariana. It was like her words were battering rams, each one striking the girl until her eyes clouded over and she shook her head. She rinsed the glass she was washing, set it too hard on a folded towel, where it bumped against another, which toppled over and created a domino effect. Chelsea dived to save glasses from crashing against the floor. Mariana's hands flew up to her face as she watched in horror.

Chelsea expected Aimee to scream or gasp, but what she did was worse. *"Fuera de aqui,"* she said in a deadly quiet voice, firing the girl on the spot.

Holding her jeans up around her waist with one hand while dabbing at her eyes with the other, Mariana fled the room.

"Daisy, don't just stand there, clean up that mess!" Aimee demanded as she stormed after Mariana. "I have a call to make!"

By the time Chelsea had disposed of the debris and Aimee returned, the dishes were all washed and put away.

"Can you believe that brat?" Aimee said as she sat down.

"I think someone hit her earlier. She seemed kind of afraid or nervous—"

"Give me a break," Aimee said. "Someone got exasperated with her and I don't blame them."

"But hitting—"

"I can't abide busybodies," Aimee interrupted with a warning scowl. "I sure hope you aren't one. Now, how about some iced tea?"

"No thank you," Chelsea said.

"Tea for me, Daisy, not for you," Aimee said.

"Oh." Chelsea found a pitcher of tea in the fridge and poured a glass. Aiming to get the conversation back on track, she delivered the iced glass with a question. "I see another house is being built up the road. Are you going to have neighbors?"

"That's my new place," Aimee said. "This house is so dated and small. And it reminds me of Devin. That's my husband."

"Oh. I take it you're divorced or—"

"No," she interrupted. "He was framed and sent to jail. I'm going to tear this place down and build an indoor tennis court. I love it up here. Oh, everyone thought Devin was the driving force behind buying this land, but it was really me."

"You must be livid at the people who put your husband in prison," Chelsea said.

"Do you know what he did?"

"No," Chelsea lied.

"You'll hear soon enough. People love to talk."

"Don't you resent the people who, um, accused him or testified against him?" Chelsea said, still trying to get a response to her question.

"The main rat behind it was my sexy bodyguard," Aimee said in a confidential tone. "What a hunk, but Devin should have known better than to hire someone as straight-arrow as him. I can't tell you how often I pranced around in next to nothing and he never made a move." She thrust out a lower lip. "Don't you have something you need to do?"

Everything about this woman grated on Chelsea's

nerves. She wore entitlement like a badge of honor, as though it was something she'd earned. The sneer beneath her smile and smirk lingering in her eyes bore this out. And if there was an ounce of compassion or humanity in her, it was well-hidden. "Yes, ma'am," Chelsea murmured as she began wiping down a counter.

Aimee gave no sign that she'd noticed Chelsea's sarcasm. She tapped her fingernails against the windowsill as she sipped the tea. In contrast to her afternoon ensemble of shorts and a cotton blouse, she currently wore a plunging white jumpsuit. High-heeled sandals gave her a two-inch lift, aided by mounds of reddish brown hair piled atop her head. She was a pretty thirty-something-year-old woman living all alone on a mesa.

"On a different subject," Chelsea began, "since I really only have tomorrow to plan and shop for Friday night, I need a few details about your soiree."

"My what?"

"Soiree. Party."

"What details?"

"Like who's invited."

"My guests enjoy their privacy."

"Well, that's great but I need some idea of quantity and allergies…"

She waved her hand. "We can discuss all that tomorrow when you whip a few things up. Actually, I'm glad I ran into you. I'm having a breakfast meeting in the morning. Maria can't cook worth a lick so I'll have to depend on you to have a carafe of hot coffee in the garden room at six thirty, followed by breakfast at seven."

"Okay," Chelsea said. "What are your menu preferences?"

"Oh, anything. Eggs benedict with smoked salmon, biscuits, pancakes, sliced fruit—you know, the usual."

As Chelsea's idea of the usual was apparently a bagel, she only nodded. Aimee's cell phone rang and she slipped it from an invisible pocket, checked the screen and swiped it on. "About time you called," she said, as she walked out of the room. "Where are you?"

Chelsea thought about eavesdropping on Aimee's side of the conversation but abandoned the idea. Instead she let herself outside onto a narrow porch. A closed gate on her left invited investigation and she opened it cautiously. It was dark by now, but as she moved inside the gate, sensors activated low-wattage lights that illuminated a footpath that led to a spacious patio.

Several rooms of the house bordered the patio. One was brightly lit and drew her attention. She saw Aimee perched on the corner of a desk in a room that was decidedly masculine. Her husband's old den or office? Maybe. She was still on her phone.

The path curved around a built-in grill and toward a lovely pool. Native rock and clever use of the land's natural contours made what had to be an aboveground pool appear like a sunken one. It would be heaven to jump in and paddle around but she knew without asking that was a no-no for the hired help. She walked around the pool and let herself out through another gate.

All pretense of prettiness disappeared. This was the utility part of the property, the place where garbage was collected and yard tools were scattered. Its dominant feature was a small building from which the tantalizing aroma of chili wafted on a welcome breeze. A clothesline with various female garments hung on it ran between the structure and a fence. Since the front door was ajar, Chelsea craned her neck to see if this was where Mariana had disappeared to, but the only person she saw was a woman fanning herself with a magazine.

She continued walking until the trail split, the left leading to some weathered-looking buildings a good distance away, and the right toward the bluff.

The wind grew stronger as she reached the guardrail that kept unwary pedestrians from walking too close to the edge. She perched atop it and rested one hand on her abdomen. Her new short hair blew around her face in a pleasant way.

She counted back in her head, wondering how "old" she was in this rendition of her life without a past. Day one would be the crash. Day two would be Doc Fisher. Day three, her brother, day four, the day she bolted and that made today day five. In those five days she'd traveled from California to Nevada to Arizona, shot two men, killing one, been cold, hot, terrified and lost in rapture. Not bad for the first five days of "life."

She turned her attention to the valley below. From this vantage point, she could see the town in the distance and the more or less straight road that led between it and the mesa, obvious because of the moving headlights of vehicles traveling north and south. Many other lights twinkled, indicating occupied homes, but the brightest glow came from Hard Rock.

"I thought I might find you out here," a man said,

Recognizing the voice, she smiled as she turned. Adam settled his hands on her shoulders, leaned down and kissed the top of her head. It felt so right to have him near. Safer, too, though that was an odd thought as nothing remotely dangerous had happened since they'd gotten to Arizona.

Which must mean they'd fallen off their nemesis' radar.

"Aren't you supposed to be rousting rowdy teenagers?" she asked.

"Not until later," he said, sitting on the fence beside her. "Aren't you supposed to be cooking something?"

"Not until later," she mimicked with a smile. "Tonight all I accomplished was getting a girl fired."

"Why do you say that?"

She told him about Mariana's upsetting departure from the kitchen. "She has a bruised cheek. Do you think Aimee's capable of hitting her?"

"Aimee is impetuous, self-centered and impatient, so, yes, it's possible she lost her temper," he said. "How about this party? Who's coming?"

"She isn't saying. Claims people want their privacy. And why can't anybody who works in her house speak much English?"

Adam considered her question. "It might be a holdover from her husband wanting everything he said and did to be a secret. It came out in the trial that he was also importing drugs. Maybe she got used to his ways. She's very fluent in Spanish. Have you discovered yet that you know some of the language, too?"

"I overheard two women talking to each other and

actually knew what they were saying. But Aimee talks too fast for me."

"Where is she now?" Adam asked.

"Aimee? Inside. She's all dressed up like she's going out, but the last I saw she was talking with someone on the phone."

"A broken date?"

"I have no idea."

"Man, we have nothing."

"Well, she did mention a six thirty a.m. meeting tomorrow."

He perked up. "Did she say with whom?"

"A business associate."

"What kind of business associate?"

"She didn't say."

He swore under his breath. "Diego told me Aimee is behind in paying his crew's wages. I wonder why."

"Knowing Aimee for all of two hours, I can say with some authority that if she thought yanking their chains would amuse her, she would do just that. She likes power."

He stared at her. "You think so?"

"Oh, yeah."

"I wish I knew if the boyfriend is Tom Nolan," Adam said. "I never noticed the two of them cozying up to each other while Holton was around, but then again, she had a husband and he had a wife to consider. Still, he's the kind of older, suave guy that Aimee might be drawn to."

"What does he look like?"

"About fifty, a silver ponytail and a diamond stud in his left ear. You'll know him if you see him."

"You said he was a crony of Holton's," Chelsea said. "Are you thinking he might still be doing Holton's bidding?"

"In other words, orchestrating these attacks on me? Yeah, that's what I'm thinking. Maybe he lost a bundle when Holton was arrested so he has a stake in retribution. This is all guesswork, of course. Everything seems to be." He pulled Chelsea to her feet but didn't release her hands. "Almost everything, that is. Right now, you're the one sure thing in my life."

And he was the only reality in hers. It had been a long, long day. Chelsea allowed herself to be coaxed into his arms. It felt wonderful to be pressed against his chest and when he kissed her, she didn't pull away. His hands slid down her back, where his caresses awakened the lust that was never buried very deep when he was near. "How about a moonlight tour of my new home away from home?" he whispered.

She'd be a hypocrite to deny she wanted him, but wanting and taking were two different things. If she gave in now, she would weaken her resolve to stay at arm's length until this situation was resolved and her memory returned. She knew she should push his hands away, but he'd reached under her blouse and his fingers stroking her bare skin seared her with pleasure.

As the tip of his tongue teased apart her lips, he cupped her breast. She ran her hands beneath his shirt, passing over the small bandage that protected the knife wound, before gliding over the smooth ridges of his defined abs. She longed to feel his bare skin press down on hers…

"We need to take this someplace private," he said, his lips moving against hers, his breathing heavy.

She summoned willpower. It took a second, but finally she placed her hands on either side of his head and looked up at him.

"We have to stop," she whispered.

"Chelsea, I love you, you know that."

She nodded. But she knew he must have said those same words when he asked her to marry him. The next day he'd disappeared without a word to her. So, really, what did love mean?

"There isn't anything I wouldn't do."

"I know. But I need space, I told you that."

He dropped his arms and turned toward the bluff. After a second, he turned back to her as he plucked his phone from his pocket. "I have to make a call. Why don't you go inside? I'll see you tomorrow."

She looked past him toward the valley. "What's that orange glow near the highway? Is that a fire?"

He nodded as he spoke into the phone.

"Look at the speed it's spreading," she said, almost mesmerized, but also suddenly anxious, as though fire licked at her feet. The breeze drove the flames that now seemed to race exponentially faster as they headed from the road back up the land toward an illuminated building.

She touched Adam's arm. "I hear sirens," she said.

"So do I." He clicked off his phone. "They put me on hold. Half the valley is probably reporting this."

"Do you know what's burning?"

"I passed a parched field this afternoon when I drove up here," he told her. "If it's the same place, I think there's an old abandoned barn up where it's headed. But there are houses and other buildings near that one as well as bushes and trees."

They fell silent as the sirens grew louder and flashing lights appeared on the highway.

Chelsea heard a sound behind them and turned around to face the house. Even from this distance, she was able to discern Aimee's lithe figure, illuminated under the outdoor lights, hurrying from the front of the house to the nearby garage, where she disappeared inside. A moment later, an engine roared to life and she drove off down the road. "Aimee just left," she said softly.

Adam turned. "I wonder where she's going?"

"Maybe to make up with the boyfriend."

"Driving alone? She usually has Miguel drive her."

"Who's Miguel?"

"He works here, or at least he used to. Aimee is going to get caught in traffic if she heads toward Hard Rock." He swore, then added, "I should have been ready to trail her and see where she's headed and who she meets." He looked down at Chelsea, his eyes little more than glistening pools. "I got distracted."

"Don't blame your inattention on me," she said with a smile. "You started it."

He kissed her forehead. "Don't worry, I know who's at fault. But trust me, the next time that woman leaves this place by herself, I'm going to be right behind her."

As the sirens grew louder they turned back to gaze

at the fire, which had doubled in size and now seemed to light up the night. Traffic had all but stopped as cars pulled off the highway to watch. A few human figures, illuminated by the flames, appeared on the burned-out edges of the field. The fire trucks finally pulled onto the property while the fire kept spreading. Police cars now raced down the highway, blue lights pulsing like an anxious heart. Chelsea shivered. She could almost feel heat in the smoke.

Adam wrapped his arm around her shoulders. "Are you afraid?" he asked softly.

"Not for myself, no, but the people down there are so vulnerable..."

"I know."

THEY WATCHED THE fire burn until the last flame died away. Before that happened, the fire had jumped into a few trees and from there to rooftops. They'd witnessed two ambulances arrive and eventually depart. Chelsea had been crying for the past ten minutes. Not sobbing, just tears rolling down her cheeks.

He knew a very dark memory caused her tears even though she didn't. He'd tried to protect her by getting her to leave the bluff when he first spotted the fire, but that hadn't worked. Was it possible the fire affected her so deeply because it stirred one of her darkest memories? Might that be a sign other memories, hopefully more pleasant ones, would start returning?

"We've escaped death at least three times in the last five days," she said as she leaned in against him. They watched as the ambulances' taillights raced back to town, their sirens heralding the journey. "I hope those people are half as lucky as we've been."

"I do, too," he said and wished with all his heart that he could spend the night comforting her. He wanted to fall asleep with her in his arms and wake up with her in the morning. He wanted to be there if the fire brought nightmares and she needed him.

But that was not to be. She was dazed and worn by smoke and events, and he had vandals to go find.

"Aimee still hasn't come home," she commented.

He settled his arm around her shoulders. "She could be caught in that mess down below. Come on, I'll escort you back to the house. It's time for me to go watch for some stupid kids."

Eventually, after a quick shower to wash off the stench of smoke, he found himself a concealed spot created by the turn of the deck and a cantilevered window. The night had finally cooled off and he knew that it would be downright cold before long. Tonight he'd observe. Tomorrow he would borrow Diaz's phone and tomorrow night, he would capture them in the act, whatever that turned out to be.

Maybe viewing a good incriminating photograph with their parents looking over their shoulders might be all the dissuasion the kids needed.

The most noteworthy thing that happened was that Aimee's car—at least he assumed it was hers—arrived back on the mesa at one thirty. By three o'clock, shivering in his T-shirt and literally unable to keep his eyes open another moment, he gave up on the vandals. Maybe they'd gotten caught up in the traffic out on the highway. He needed to get some sleep if he was going to function tomorrow. He walked back to his modest trio of rooms and let himself in. He was asleep two minutes after his head hit the pillow.

Chapter Fourteen

Chelsea dared only glance at Aimee's early morning visitor, a well-built guy packed into a blue T-shirt decorated with a setting sun. His back was to the room and he didn't turn as she settled the heavy tray on a round table by the window.

He did not have silver hair in a ponytail, nor could she see a diamond stud. The guy was not Tom Nolan.

It wasn't until he grumbled something, paused, then spoke again that Chelsea realized he was on the phone.

"Where are the pancakes?" Aimee demanded right as the man on the phone finally started speaking.

Chelsea jerked to attention. She gestured at one of the plates. "Right here."

"They look funny."

"They're johnnycakes."

"That's cornmeal, right? Did I ask for cornmeal? I hate the stuff."

Chelsea had had a miserable night and Aimee's complaints irritated the heck out of her. "I'll just pour the juice," she said.

"I can pour my own damn juice." Aimee turned to the man who had just ended his call. "Davy? Breakfast."

He pocketed his phone and turned to face them. His friendly, tanned face, blue eyes and straight teeth seemed to indicate he was a guy who would stay young-looking into middle age. "It smells great," he said as he brushed long hair off his forehead. "I'm starving."

Aimee was obviously still distressed about something. "Maybe I should cancel the party," she told him.

Davy poured a glass of juice and handed it to her. "Calm down, everything is going to work out. We need the party, the noise, the distraction. Now drink this, you'll feel better." He wrapped his arm around her. "Besides, I have a plan."

"Like what?" she asked then seemed to remember Chelsea. "Are you actually eavesdropping on us?" she snapped.

"No… I—"

"Close the door on your way out."

Chelsea fought the urge to curtsy and headed for the door.

"Thanks for the food," Davy called as she left the room.

This was the boyfriend? Well, maybe it took someone as laid-back as him to cope with Aimee's mercurial moods. More importantly, Chelsea still had no idea what the meeting had been about. The only two words she'd managed to glean from Davy's phone conversation were *trouble* and *adjustments* and they seemed appropriate for any business situation.

When Chelsea started to pack up the leftovers she

suspected Aimee would never eat, she had a better idea. She filled another tray and took it out to the small house she'd seen the night before. Surely someone out there could eat this food. She was also hoping for a chance to talk to Mariana.

Her brisk knock was answered by the woman whom she'd seen fanning herself the night before. Her lovely eyes widened as she scanned the huge tray of goodies Chelsea held in front of her.

"I'm the new cook. I brought, well, food." This was said in English with a few words of Spanish thrown in, but the woman, who shared that her name was Sofia, apparently understood. Although she looked wary about accepting the tray, she unburdened Chelsea. *"Gracias,"* she murmured.

"Is Mariana here?" Chelsea added.

Sofia frowned. "Mariana?"

"About fifteen, maybe sixteen. Long hair."

Sofia shook her head. "I don't know…"

"You mean she never stayed here?"

"No."

"Maybe another building—"

"There is only the men's building," Sofia insisted. "That's where my husband, Miguel, lives. I would know if there was a girl there." This last comment was accompanied by a shy smile.

"I see. Well, okay then. I—I hope you enjoy the food."

"I'll share it with Miguel," she said.

A young married couple living apart? Could she stand being that close to Adam and not in the same bed? Judging by the bad dreams that had plagued her last night, the answer was no.

Instead of heading back to the house, Chelsea turned toward the bluff. As she walked, she thought about Mariana. If the girl had been working for Aimee for any length of time, wouldn't Sofia have heard of her? Even if she'd never stayed overnight on the mesa, Chelsea thought Sofia would have seen her. Where was Mariana?

The view from the bluff stunned Chelsea. Acres of blackened land, burned-out buildings and ravaged trees covered a large swath. How had the people the ambulances evacuated fared? Tears once again burned her eyes. The fire had haunted her sleep, had filled her dreams. She had no idea why it bothered her so much. There'd been flames during the attack at Bill's place and they'd frozen her for a heartbeat, but they hadn't tortured her this way.

She returned to the house to find Maria hard at work. As Chelsea joined in to clean the kitchen, she wondered if she should drop the pretense of not understanding or speaking much Spanish so she could ask a few pertinent questions. Tomorrow, she decided, unless Aimee fired her first. Maria left the kitchen when the work was done.

With tomorrow's party in mind, Chelsea grabbed a pencil and paper and started making a list. Pool parties equaled buffet in her mind. The grocery list of appetizers, vegetarian shish kebabs and seafood skewers grew as the menu came together.

With the vision of the scorched valley still on her

mind, Chelsea switched on the small television built into the cabinetry, hoping to get news about the fire. She flipped through several channels before catching the tail end of an interview obviously filmed at a hospital.

"All we can do for my dad now is pray," a distraught-looking man said right into the camera.

The camera switched to a woman reporter standing in front of a burned-out building. "Again, to recap," she said, "Wednesday night at nine thirty-five, Hard Rock Fire Department responded to a grass fire on Hanson Road. One man is dead, another hospitalized for third-degree burns. Both men are thought to have been trapped in their respective homes. The fire burned about twenty acres of grassland along with several buildings. Though still under investigation, sources report it's suspected a burning cigarette thrown from a car is the cause. Stay tuned to Channel—"

Chelsea turned off the TV. The expression in the man's eyes as he talked about his father filled her head and she suddenly understood what it was that struck a chord in her heart with him and with Mariana. She'd lived with the same thing day and night since Adam had pulled her from the helicopter, and last night when the fire in the valley looked like a flowing river of lava, she'd felt it cut to her very quick.

Fear. They were both very, very afraid.

ADAM AWOKE TO a knock on his door. He pulled on his jeans and answered it to find Diego Diaz standing on the threshold with a cinnamon roll wrapped in a napkin and a mug of coffee grasped in his other hand.

"Hey, Frank, thought you might need something to eat," he said as he handed Adam breakfast.

"Thanks," Adam said, taking a grateful sip of coffee. "I'm afraid the kids didn't show up last night."

"Yeah, nothing's missing, no new insults. The fire must have kept them away."

"The fire was terrible. Do you know if anyone was hurt?"

"One man dead," Diaz said, "and one in the hospital. I live about a quarter mile from him. Jim's an okay guy, I hope he makes it."

"Did your house—?"

"Some smoke, nothing else."

"I need a favor," Adam said before Diaz left. "This is none of my business, I know that, but yesterday you mentioned the boss is holding the crew's wages back."

Diego shook his head. "I'm paying you myself, you don't need to worry about that, Frank. Ms. Holton has some cash-flow issue or something. She'll come through and I'll get my money back. Anything else?"

"Yeah, I need to borrow your camera tonight. I want to catch those kids in the act."

"Won't they see your flash or hear the noise it makes?"

"I'm betting on it. They'll run like scared dogs."

"What if they turn on you?"

Adam smiled. "Don't worry about it."

"Dude…don't hurt them," Diego said, eyes narrowed.

"Please, I'm an ex-cop. Maybe you can share the photo with their folks and avoid the police altogether."

"Good idea. I have an extra phone in the glove box.

I'll leave it before I go home. Don't worry if you're busy, I have a key."

"Thanks."

After Diaz left, Adam ate the cinnamon roll and drank the coffee. He quickly dressed and walked toward the Holton house. In a garden shed, he found an unattended straw hat and some clippers. Thus camouflaged, he staked out a rambling bush next to the house. A big SUV was parked close to Aimee's front door and he quickly memorized the plate, though he'd have to get Whip to check it out as he had no pull with the police. After pretending to be a gardener for over an hour, the door opened and a man about his own age exited the house.

To Adam, the emerging man didn't look like Aimee's type in that he didn't look wealthy or connected. Just a guy who hung out at the beach, but hell, maybe she was tired of movers and shakers and felons and villains.

The car pulled away and Adam remained at his post, trying to figure out a way to get in the house to see Chelsea. He told himself it was to find out if she'd overheard anything, but the truth was he just wanted to see her.

Toward that goal, he walked quickly along the drive that jutted off behind the house, where he could see in the kitchen window. Chelsea's red hair announced her back was to the sink. It appeared she was talking to somebody he couldn't see. He waited until she faced the sink, then waved a hand until the motion caught her attention. She shook her head and turned back into the room, but a moment later, she left the sink and a moment after that, she came through the back door.

"Did you hear that someone died in the fire and another person ended up in the hospital?" she said softly as she reached his side.

He took her hand and led her to a spot where they wouldn't be visible through a window. "Yes, I did."

"I had nightmares about that fire last night," she said with a shudder. "I don't know why it got to me on such a deep level. I kept seeing an old woman in the flames. Today when I heard it was a man who died, I was actually surprised. It was so real."

He looked into her eyes. "I should have told you last night," he said. "I didn't want to upset you, but I can see now my silence didn't help. Chelsea, your grandmother died in a fire when you were twelve. You adored her, she was a constant in your life because your mom was at the tavern working so much—anyway, her death devastated you."

"My grandmother." She swallowed hard. "I don't remember her. What was her name?"

"Ann, same as your middle name."

"I want so much to remember her. Well, at least it explains the tears and the dreams—oh, my gosh, Adam. Does this mean my subconscious memory is returning?"

"I don't know. The fire at Bill's didn't get to you like this, but on the other hand, you were fighting for your life."

"It was different this time, more profound. I must be getting better. I hope so."

"So do I." He hugged her close, relishing the smell of her hair and the feel of her body next to his. But he could also feel the restraint in her embrace.

"Where are you staying in the house?" he asked. "Which room is yours?"

She pointed to the windows a little distance from the kitchen. "My room is right there. Why?"

"I don't know for sure. I just want to know where you are. Did you get a guest list for tomorrow's party? What did you learn about the business meeting this morning? Did—?"

"You want a rundown?" she interrupted as she held up a closed fist. "Okay, here goes," She raised a finger. "One, Aimee almost canceled her party but don't ask me why. Two, she is in a foul mood. I don't think she got much sleep last night. Three, Miguel is going to man the grill."

"Then he's still here. Good."

"I met his wife earlier. Her name is Sofia."

"They got married? How about that! Okay, continue."

"Four, no guest list, just forty or so unidentified people who are on their own when it comes to any allergies because Aimee can't be bothered to ask them. Let's see, her visitor this morning used the words *trouble* and *adjustments* while on the phone. I don't know if he's just a business associate or a boyfriend."

"Did he look like a surfer dude?'

She nodded.

"I saw him leave. Did you get a name?"

"Davy."

"Not much help there. Anything else?"

She thought for a second. "Let's see. The party people called to say that they couldn't get here to decorate the patio until tomorrow, which set Aimee off big-time." She held up the other hand. "A refrigerator for the new house is being delivered this afternoon and that has Aimee spitting nails because it's not supposed to come for another two months and now it's got to be stored in the shop or shed or something way off down that way."

"The new shed."

"Yeah. Lastly, Aimee is headed off to the spa pretty soon. That's all I've got." She smiled and added, "It's getting late and I have a ton of shopping to do for the party. Want to drive into Hard Rock with me? I could use the company."

"Sounds good, but I think I should follow Aimee. I'm also going to meet Dennis later on today. Take the teenager you told me about last night. Maybe you can ferret out how she got the bruise."

"Mariana's whereabouts are currently a mystery. I'll manage."

He grasped her shoulders and gently kissed her lips. "I'll check the oil in the van, then I'd better get ready to trail Aimee. Love you," he added, noting the anxious look in her eyes as he uttered the words. Well, she could hem and haw all she wanted, his feelings were crystal clear.

He waited for Aimee to leave the property from behind the cover of the guard shack. When she finally drove by in her white convertible, he gave her a few minutes to get ahead so the sound of his motorcycle wouldn't draw her attention. Once she hit Hard Rock city limits, she slowed down and turned off Main Street, traversing small roads to the seedier side of the city. It surprised the hell out of him when she pulled into a motel parking lot. The place was definitely not her style, but she got out of her car, quickly approached one of the outside doors, knocked, scanned the area around her as though looking to see if anyone was watching, and scurried inside when the door opened.

Interesting.

Two hours later, Tom Nolan walked out of the room with a smug grin on his tanned face. He ambled out of the parking lot and down a side street, where he got behind the wheel of a black Mercedes and drove off. Aimee didn't appear for another thirty minutes. No sauntering for her. Huge sunglasses partially concealed her face as she scanned her surroundings and practically ran to her car. He followed her to the ritzy part of town. She handed her keys to a valet and entered her favorite spa, where he knew from experience she would linger for hours.

So Tom Nolan was the boyfriend and the guy from the morning, Davy something, was just a business associate? What business, and did either man have anything to do with the attacks on him and Chelsea?

Why had the attacks stopped? The reasonable explanation was that no one knew where they were. While it was nice not to be shot at or to have Chelsea threatened, it seemed the momentum of their situation had ground to a halt.

And that meant that now was the time to keep alert and not become complacent. Whip was right, sooner or later, Dennis would tell someone he'd seen Adam or Adam would be spotted again—it was inevitable that something would tip someone off. Sooner or later the "bad guys" would be back on their trail. This was his opportunity to get to them before they got to him.

Maybe he'd have to depend on Whip after all.

He drove to the taco truck to meet Dennis, his thoughts now centered on the mysterious box. He found the place more crowded than usual and alive with music thanks to the efforts of a three-man band set up on a makeshift stage. People swayed to their country beat, occasionally dropping a dollar or two into the band's open guitar case as the taco truck did a booming business.

Good grief. Could he have chosen a more public spot to center his activities in Hard Rock? This was the absolute last time he was coming near this place. He took off his helmet but kept his cap pulled low on his face and his sunglasses in place.

A man walking across the grass caught his attention. There was something about the way he moved—a little stutter in his gait. He wore slacks and a sports shirt. A baseball cap covered most of his head, but a few strands of auburn hair showed down by his neck. The guy looked over his shoulder as he approached the alley that ran behind the taco truck and Adam glimpsed his profile. In that instant, he knew who he was looking at.

US Marshal Ron Ballard, here in Arizona, just like Whip had predicted.

Adam waited until Ballard focused his attention back on the alley and then he began threading his way through the jostling crowd, the confusion created by the loud music masking his movement. He caught one last glimpse of Ballard before he turned a corner and disappeared into the alley. Adam broke into a trot until he stopped near the corner. He checked to make sure no one was watching him, then retrieved his gun and turned the corner carefully in case he was being set up for an ambush.

The alley was heavily shadowed. Adam tore off the sunglasses and spotted Ballard fifty feet ahead of him walking toward the light at the far end. He picked up his pace as he followed the man, reviewing his options as he moved between shadows. Without a vehicle at hand, he couldn't trail Ballard. He needed to confront him. Why was the guy here? Was it like Whip had said, that Adam was a loose end? And most important, who was Ballard working for?

Adam left the shadows to stand in the center of the alley, gun still at his side. "Ballard!" he yelled.

The marshal turned but with his back to the light, Adam couldn't read his expression. A sudden laugh jarred Adam. "Is that you, Parish?" Ballard called, sounding anything but happy. "I knew you weren't really dead, you jerk. Do you know what trouble you've caused me? I wish you had gone down with your plane, at least then I wouldn't have to—"

Ballard's hand suddenly rocketed up from his side. A single shot erupted from behind Adam, so he threw himself to the ground, aware as he did so that Ballard had crumpled to the pavement where he stood. Adam turned his head to find Whip standing several yards behind him, his arm still held out in front, his gun gripped in his hand.

Lowering his weapon, the older man immediately walked up to Adam and extended a hand to help him to his feet. "Are you okay?"

"I'm—I'm fine," Adam stuttered. "I'm…wait. Why did you shoot—?"

"He drew on you," Whip interrupted. "I aimed to wound him so he could tell us who's behind all this… I don't know, though, I was kind of rushed." Whip strode toward the fallen man, Adam right on his heels.

Ballard was lying on the pavement, a Glock 23-caliber pistol clutched in his right hand. "See?" Whip said, gesturing at the Glock. His voice sounded a little relieved. No cop liked shooting an unarmed man.

Adam kneeled to check for a pulse. "He's gone."

"Damn. I'm sorry, son."

Adam kept his gaze on Ballard's body as he stood. "I saw him raise his hand but I didn't see the gun," he said as he met Whip's gaze. "If you hadn't been here… How *did* you happen to be in this alley?"

"Ballard was waiting for me after my interview," Whip said. "He started asking me a lot of questions about you. There was something off about him. I got the feeling he knew you were in Hard Rock so I decided to find out where he went next. My heart almost stopped when I saw you follow him into this alley."

Adam shook his head, still dumbfounded by Ballard's presence in Arizona and by the finality of the man's death. "You better call this in," he said.

"I'm not calling in anything until you get out of town," Whip said.

Adam shook his head. "I'm not leaving—"

"This isn't your decision. This is self-defense with or without your involvement. What with him being a Marshal and me being a cop, none of this will hit the news until the facts are known. Once Ballard's activities are exposed, there won't be a problem for me, trust me. Now go so I can start the ball rolling."

"But—"

"No, Adam, now listen to me. Think about Chelsea. You don't know that Ballard didn't already tell Devin Holton's goons he found you, there could be a new attack coming any minute. She'll be a sitting duck if you get caught up in this, too. There are so few ways I can help you but this I can do. Go. Get Chelsea, get out of Hard Rock for good."

Adam nodded as he tucked away his gun. It went against the grain to walk away but Whip was right. As soon as Adam got involved with the police, Chelsea would be left high and dry. He looked Whip in the eyes. "I don't know when I'll see you again—"

"Don't get all touchy-feely on me," the older man said, then gave him a spontaneous hug.

Adam walked away. As he crossed the park, he tried calling Dennis but the call went immediately to voice mail. He rode out of town but not before making one fast stop at a small store, where he bought Chelsea a prepaid phone of her own. She needed a way to call for help should the occasion arise.

By the time he got back to the mesa, the sun was

well on its way down and the construction crew was long gone. He stopped off at his place to leave the bike so he could hike up the road.

When he got close to the house, he heard music coming from the patio. Past experience at this house told him Aimee was out by the pool and that meant he could chance going around back to see Chelsea. Her welcoming smile went a long way toward easing his anxiety and she pulled him inside without hesitation.

"I take it Aimee is on the patio?"

"For the time being," Chelsea said. The kitchen smelled wonderful. Trays of pretty little food lined the drain boards while the sink was filled with piles of dirty dishes. She was in her element and it brightened her eyes and flushed her cheeks a beguiling pink.

"We have to talk," he said as he snatched a shrimp and popped it in his mouth.

"These are the test hors d'oeuvres. Aimee is coming in soon to choose what she likes."

He swiped another shrimp, and then told her about Ballard.

"Dead?" she whispered. "Thank God Whip was there."

"I know. He'll still have to go through an investigation, though. Without a witness and with the other gun unfired—"

"He told you he'd take care of it," Chelsea said. "Let him. If you have to come in later to make things right, you can."

"We have to leave tonight—"

"No," she said immediately. "Not tonight. Not until after the party."

"But—"

"Just because the guy who fingered you is dead doesn't mean you're out of danger. The deal was to find out the truth. I know it sounds silly, but I have a feeling about tomorrow night, Adam. Something is going to happen at that party, I know it in my bones. Something that tells you exactly who is behind what."

He had the same feeling and it probably was silly. But neither Whip nor the police knew he was on this mesa—if he stayed out of sight until Saturday morning, they should both be fine. "Okay," he said.

She handed him a little biscuit with flecks of prosciutto baked in the dough. Heaven. "Did you see Dennis?" she asked. "I've been dying to know what's in the box."

"I missed Dennis."

"Shoot. Well, how about Aimee. Who did she meet?"

"Tom Nolan and at a motel no less. Probably because of his wife."

"I overheard her on the phone a little while ago. It sounded like she was talking to her father and she was asking for money. I think Aimee may have stretched herself too thin."

"That explains the paycheck thing," Adam said.

"And judging from the way she threw her phone after she disconnected, I don't think Daddy said yes."

"Speaking of phones," Adam said and produced the new one he'd bought her. When they heard a door close somewhere in the house, it was time for him to go.

She pressed a napkin filled with appetizers into his hands. "Hurry," she said, "I hear footsteps."

"Call me later, okay?"

"I don't know your number."

"I programmed it into the phone. Call me. I miss you."

"I miss you, too," she whispered and sounded as though she meant it.

His phone rang as Adam patrolled the deck. Half expecting a call from Whip, he was pleased to hear Chelsea's voice.

What she didn't know, couldn't remember, were the hundreds of calls they'd made to one another. Some people fell in love over endless texts and emails but he and Chelsea had used the phone, craving the sound of one another's voices, discussing their days and dreaming about what was to come. Sometimes they'd spend the whole day and evening together and still find things to talk about in midnight calls.

And so it was tonight. Was it a pipe dream to think she might fall in love with him again even if her memory never returned? As for him, the sound of her voice transported him to her side. But eventually, he had to remind her to stay around other people the next day, that he was going to find Dennis and retrieve the box. He made her promise to call him if anything alarmed her. When he heard an approaching vehicle, he ended the call. He stood up and dug Diego's camera out of his pocket.

What if it wasn't the vandals? What if this was the beginning of another attack on him and Chelsea?

He moved down the path toward the clearing, careful to stay out of the moonlight, gun drawn.

It sounded like the vehicle stopped out by the construction office, out of view of where he lurked. He heard doors open and close, then male voices, adult voices, and he tensed. "Where is it?" someone said.

"I think we turned too early. Didn't they say the second right? It's up the road."

"Man, we're so late."

"That engine trouble wasn't our fault. At least we can still make today's deadline if we deliver before twelve. Don't forget the bonus."

"But we still have to unload—"

"Stop whining. It's up the road, I'm sure of it. Look, you can see lights."

"I can't believe we have to drive back to Phoenix tonight," the complainer grumbled as the sound of opening and closing doors reached Adam's ears. The vehicle soon continued up the mesa toward the main house. By the position of the headlamps, it appeared to be a truck.

That had to be the refrigerator people and the delivery bonus had to be huge to justify these hours. He walked back to the house and leaned against an outside wall, where he could look down at the valley below. Thirty minutes later the delivery truck bounced and squeaked its way back down the hill, refrigerator apparently signed, sealed and delivered.

He walked around the house a few times, something made possible because of the 360 degree deck. Were those kids ever going to show? This was the last night he planned on waiting out here—a lot of good he'd done Diaz construction.

Forty minutes passed before the bass beat of a rap song and skidding brakes announced more visitors. Adam was once again alert for someone with worse intent than vandalism. Doors slammed, high-pitched giggles erupted. A thud announced someone had fallen and the subsequent slurred warning to be quiet made Adam certain he was listening to three or four drunk kids.

Was the driver sober?

Pounding footsteps ran toward the house, slowing down when the vandals reached the front deck and entered the semi-skeletal structure. Judging from discernable shapes, there were three of them and they could barely stand up straight. One held a can above his head and shook it, the sound of the marble rattling inside the can disturbing the still night air. The kid staggered around a bit before he randomly sprayed. The other two followed suit, weaving their way around the structure, pausing to spray when the mood hit them.

Adam took a few pictures of them through the window opening and caught the open beer bottles each was holding. They were so preoccupied they didn't even notice the flash. Tiptoeing off his perch on the deck, he made his way up the trail, using the flashlight on the phone to check out the truck while keeping his senses alert for any trouble that might come from Holton's direction.

He found no additional teens, drunk or sober. He opened the hood and took the distributor cap, then closed it. He strode off the road to another concealed spot behind a couple of tall bushes and called Diego. It was answered on the second ring.

"What?" Diego responded abruptly, though his voice was fuzzy because he'd been woken up.

"This is Adam. Get on up here ASAP."

"Now?"

"Yep. The kids are here and they're too drunk to drive. I disabled their truck, but you need to be the one to call the police."

"I'll be there in fifteen minutes," Diego said.

"Make it ten. And don't forget the cops."

Adam waited around until Diego showed up in his dark truck, lights and engine off, momentum carrying the heavy vehicle to a rolling stop. A shadowy Diego exited like a sooty ghost. Adam disengaged himself from the bushes and approached Diego.

"I called the police on the way up the hill," Diego whispered.

"They took a six-pack down there with them," Adam said. "Every once in a while I hear glass breaking." He gave Diego the distributor cap and the phone. "It's up to you now."

"Thanks. You'd better go."

Adam clapped the other man on the back and took off at a trot. He'd taken care of Diego's problem.

Would that his own could be so easily resolved.

Chapter Fifteen

Chelsea was up bright and early. She'd done some of the prep work for the party yesterday, but there was still a ton to do. Maria was there to help and that was nice, but as Maria's English seemed nonexistent, Chelsea found herself missing the back-and-forth banter so common in this kind of work.

Wait? How did she know what was common behavior in a commercial-like kitchen? But she did: she could remember jokes and laughing, but not faces. First the reaction to the fire, now this—was it a start? *Oh, please let it be so and let it progress quickly into memories of Adam and her family.*

Aimee showed up around ten and Maria immediately stopped helping Chelsea and served Aimee coffee and a toasted muffin. "Take it out to the patio," Aimee said as Maria approached the table with the tray. "Wait. Where's the juice and a bowl of fruit? Honestly, Maria."

"Perdón," Maria whispered.

Aimee rolled her eyes. "Daisy, have those damn party people shown up yet?"

Chelsea piled strawberries in a bowl and then froze.

She shouldn't have been able to understand Aimee's request for fruit as it was delivered in her quicksilver Spanish. But Aimee was still complaining and not paying any attention. Maria took the bowl and placed it on the tray.

"Daisy?" Aimee repeated. "The decorators? Am I alone here? What am I paying you for?"

"Catering your party," Chelsea answered as she handed a glass of juice to Maria. "And no, as far as I'm aware, the decorators haven't come yet."

Aimee got to her feet and swept out of the room. Maria followed behind her with the tray, but she glanced over at Chelsea before leaving.

When she got back, Chelsea, in Spanish, apologized for disguising the fact she understood a little Spanish.

"Don't worry about it," Maria said in perfect English.

"You lied, too?" Chelsea asked her.

Maria nodded. "Sofia worked up here before me. She's the one who told me about the job, but she said Ms. Holton wouldn't hire anyone who speaks or understands much English so I just pretended to be fresh off the boat instead of born and raised in Portland, Oregon. My family knows me as Mary Louise, but in this house, I'm Maria. Man, I about split a gut when you told the boss lady exactly what she'd hired you to do. She presumes too much."

"No kidding."

"I'm glad we can talk openly to each other," Maria said. "Sofia's husband is sick of them living apart. He wants to take off. I bunk out there during the week and if she leaves, I'll be here all alone. Maybe you could move out there with me."

"I'm not staying past tonight," Chelsea admitted. "I'm just here for this party."

"Shoot," Maria said.

"Who's coming, do you know?"

"She threw the last one for some would-be politician. I heard via Miguel that this time she's invited a TV star I've never heard of. She likes to rub shoulders."

"Were you here when Mr. Holton—?"

"No! I wouldn't work for a man like him. It's hard enough working for his wife."

"Maria, I have a question. I met a teenager here named Mariana."

"I didn't know her name," Maria said.

"Then you met her?"

"I saw her when Ms. Holton paraded her in to wash some crystal glasses. I admit it, I can be clumsy, but honestly, three glasses in nine months service? Anyway, when I spoke briefly to the girl, Ms. Holton told me to leave her be. Kind of timid, right?"

"I thought she seemed frightened and with good cause. I believe she may be a battered kid, but I'm not sure. I'd like to talk to her. Do you know where she went after Aimee sent her away?"

"Not a clue. I can ask Sofia—"

"I already asked her."

"Hopefully she went home."

Would that be any better? Not if it was her family who was abusing her. "Why do you work here if you hate it so much?" she asked Maria.

Maria shrugged. "I'm thirty-three years old. My two kids currently live with my late husband's parents in Phoenix. I'm going to college online and I'm just about done. Then I can get a job as a court reporter and get my kids back. I miss the little monsters like crazy. Aimee Holton is the means to my end."

Chelsea smiled. "I hope she's the means to my end, too," she mumbled, thinking of what Adam had said last night on the phone, that his plan was to spend the party in disguise, getting a good look at each and every guest, looking for connections to his past and to Holton. It sounded a lot easier said than done.

ADAM TRIED DENNIS'S phone first thing in the morning but there was still no answer. Since he hadn't fallen asleep until almost 4:00 a.m., it was now well after ten. That meant Dennis was undoubtedly already at work, where he wouldn't answer a personal call. Knowing Chelsea was elbow-deep in food prep and surrounded by people, he decided to drive to the old Stop and Shop in Hard Rock and see if he could catch Dennis during his lunch break.

That meant showing up in the town he'd sworn to avoid, but he had to get his hands on that box and he was wearing his trusty helmet so he was more or less invisible, right?

He found the renovation of the small grocery into a fish pet store in full swing. Several contractor vehicles were parked along the sidewalk in front while men toted supplies and tools in and out of the building. Adam pulled to the curb and waited.

At noon, the site began to clear but there was no sign of Dennis. Adam got off his bike when a burly guy with unruly eyebrows left the building and crossed the street.

"Excuse me," Adam called out, taking off his hood. "I'm looking for Dennis Woods."

"You a friend of his?"

"Yes. I've been trying to get ahold of him."

"He called in earlier. Stacy gave birth about two o'clock this morning. I guess she and the baby are both okay, but the hospital's keeping them a few days on account of it's a couple of weeks early."

"Where are the other kids?"

"Up with Stacy's sister in Phoenix."

"Thanks," Adam said as the guy moved along. What was it going to be like when Chelsea gave birth and he saw his son or daughter for the first time? Amazing, yes, but would the world suddenly look different? In a few short months, he was going to be a father and he'd find out.

God willing...

Frustration just about choked him. What would they do tomorrow morning if nothing had changed?

Suddenly Adam knew. If Chelsea agreed, he'd send her somewhere no one would ever think of looking for her and set himself up here as a target with Whip to watch his back. No more waiting around. He thought back to everything he knew about Chelsea and remembered her talking about a woman she'd met at the culinary school she'd attended in Los Angeles. They'd become friends. Sarah Miller, that was her name, and she'd taken an executive chef's position somewhere in the greater L.A. area. Chelsea wouldn't remember Sarah, but Sarah would certainly remember Chelsea, and she would also have pictures and stories.

But first there was that box Dennis had found under Adam's childhood home. He had to know what was inside. The possibility it could condemn—or clear—his father was too strong to ignore. He had to know.

The motorcycle got him to Tucson in good time and by two thirty, he'd found the hospital birthing center. He took the elevator to the second floor and walked down a nondescript hall toward the nurses' station. Before he reached it, he happened to glance through an open door into a square room and found Dennis sprawled in one of many chairs, his head flung forward, chin touching his chest, eyes closed.

Dennis looked up as Adam sat on the chair beside him. "Hey," he said in a gravelly voice.

Adam studied his friend. "You look terrible."

Dennis's smile was fleeting. "It was a long night."

"Boy or girl?"

"Boy."

"That's great, man. Congratulations."

"Thanks. He's small but perfect. The doctors say he can go home in a couple of days.

"And Stacy is okay?"

"Fine. She's asleep with the baby right now. I came down here for coffee and kind of collapsed."

Adam got up and poured his friend a cup from the carafe on the counter then sat back down.

Dennis took a long swallow. "That's good," he said, and stared at Adam a moment. "Remember our old plan?"

"You mean the tavern?"

"Yeah. You and I were going to open a place, remember? Artisanal beer, music, hire a chef and serve really excellent bar food—"

"Chelsea's a chef," Adam said. "A good one."

"Really? Well, I know all about beer and the plumbing it takes to brew it and you, my friend, can build anything."

"It would be fun. Maybe someday, who knows?" He paused for a second, then added, "I have something to tell you."

Dennis almost spit out his latest mouthful of coffee. "The box! I forgot about it. Oh, Adam, I'm sorry. I haven't even been answering the phone. You must have waited—"

"No, no, don't worry about that. My news is that I'm going to be a dad in several months. Chelsea is pregnant."

Dennis's grin was wonderful. "That's great." He slugged Adam in the arm. "Then you and her are serious?"

"Very. We're already engaged—well, it's a long story and we're doing our best to make sure it has a happy ending. I'll keep you posted."

"Fatherhood's the greatest," Dennis said. "My kids and Stacy mean the world to me."

"I can see that," Adam said. "You're an inspiration."

Dennis laughed. "I bet Whip is thrilled."

"I haven't told him," Adam said. "But you're right, he'll be excited. Anyway, about the box. If I can borrow your key I'll go get it myself."

"No need. I had already stopped at the storage garage when Stacy called and said her water broke. The box is in my car and my car is out in the parking lot."

"That's great. I'll go get it and bring your keys back."

"Maybe a walk and a breath of fresh air will revive me," Dennis said as he got to his feet and stretched. "I'll go with you."

The parking lot was out in the open and Dennis took a deep breath as they walked to his car. Their friendly catch-up chatter stopped when they found the back window of Dennis's vintage Chevy smashed. Dennis quickly stepped through the broken safety glass and unlocked the front door. He swore. "They ripped the CD player right out of the dash," he said, "Damn, that thing was brand-new!" He peered into the back seat. "Oh, Adam, shoot, your box is gone, too."

Adam stared into the empty backseat. "Maybe you put it in the trunk?" he asked hopefully.

"No, man, the trunk is full of birthday presents for our oldest." He unlocked the trunk, anyway, to reveal bags and boxes of toys.

"I'm sorry," Dennis said.

"It's not your fault."

"Yeah. First my house and now my car. What's next?"

Adam stared at the broken window and wondered the same thing.

"GONE? THE BOX IS really gone? Just like that?" Chelsea said as she juggled two trays of appetizers. The party was in full swing and Adam had just returned from Tucson. He'd spent the afternoon having Dennis's window fixed and a new CD player installed so Dennis could stay at the hospital with his wife and baby.

"Just like that," he said, relieving her of one of the trays.

"I'm sorry. You must be so disappointed."

"Yeah. He's had a couple of break-ins recently That seems really suspicious to me. Tomorrow you and I have some decisions to make and then I want to take you to the hospital to meet Stacy while I ask Dennis a little more about that box."

She agreed, pleased he was including her in his life. If they were to be married and create a family, he had to get over living like a lone wolf. But visiting friends was also such a contrast to outrunning killers that she had a hard time wrapping her head around it. Holton seemed to have a dozen henchmen willing to do his bidding. Would she and Adam live through another Nevada-scale attack?

"Anyway, that's why I'm late. What have I missed?"

Maria and Sofia came to the door. Sofia stared at Adam for a moment, then broke into a smile. "Adam? Does Miguel know you're here?"

"No, I'm kind of undercover. I haven't been around long."

"Don't let Ms. Holton see you," Sofia said, her eyes wide.

"Not on your life," he said, handing her a tray.

She nodded and hurried after Maria.

"Your Spanish is excellent," Chelsea said, proud she'd understood every word of their conversation.

"My grandmother was born and raised in Mexico City."

"I was going to say I didn't know that, but hey, that's the story of my life, right?"

He suddenly leaned over and kissed her forehead. "Okay, what did I miss today? Give me one of your famous lists."

"Let's see. According to Aimee, the contractor— your boss, right?—looked at the fancy refrigerator they delivered last night and declared it was the wrong model, so she called the store and read them the riot act. They're reordering and meanwhile, those poor delivery guys have to drive up here after work this evening and take this one back because she can't stand to have it on her property another night.

"The afternoon drama continued when the decorators didn't show up until almost four. They strung sparkle lights, strategically placed a few potted palm trees and paper lanterns, scattered flowers and presto, the patio now resembles a tropical paradise. The liquor is flowing, the television actor brought groupies and last but not least, Tom Nolan arrived."

"He's out there?"

"In the flesh. He and a jumpy Aimee exchanged a few kisses and then she reverted to a hot mess. Oh, and Nolan brought a big hulking guy instead of a wife."

"Is Davy here, too?"

"Not yet. He was here earlier when the debacle about the refrigerator was going down. I guess he had to check the numbers on the box and make sure it was indeed the wrong one. Took him forever, too. Maybe he can't read." She furrowed her brow and looked up at Adam. "I'm still expecting something to happen, something that finally helps us understand who Devin Holton designated to orchestrate your murder."

"I am, too," Adam said. "Maybe we're desperate."

"I think it's Aimee, at least for me. The first day I was here she was conceited and mean, the next day she was angry and nervous, and now she's jumping out of her skin. Something is up. What about Whip? Did you hear from him today?"

"As far as Whip knows, we're halfway to Florida so I don't expect to hear from him. There wasn't anything about it on the radio, though," he said. "Whip said they'd keep it hushed up because the guy was a US marshal." He looked longingly toward the patio, "I need to go out there and look around."

Chelsea frowned. "Maybe you could hide out in the den. It fronts the patio."

"I'll try it," he said to appease her.

"I should take more of this food out to Miguel."

"Go ahead. I know my way around this place."

ADAM FOUND THAT the den, by virtue of being the thoroughfare to the bathroom, had been decorated just like the patio, with paper lanterns strung overhead and straw hats, grass skirts and silk leis tacked to the walls. He made his way to the open glass doors and peered outside. The music was too loud to hear conversation, but Aimee and Tom Nolan had chosen to stand directly

under a string of paper lanterns and so were clearly visible. He glimpsed a burly figure behind Nolan and immediately fingered him as Nolan's bodyguard.

His attention was diverted for a moment as Chelsea
walked across the patio carrying a couple of trays she
deposited in an icebox next to the grill. She wore a red
apron that hugged her body and he fancied the slight
bulge that was his baby that had grown a little in the
past week, a fact that made him grin. She stopped to
chat for a moment with Miguel and then left the patio.

Adam shifted positions in order to change his angle
of observation, but it was no use. He would never find
out why Nolan brought along a bodyguard unless he
got out there and mingled.

Studying the patio for possible hiding places solved
nothing, but he did make an observation that gave him
an idea. Some of the guests had dressed in bright Ha-
waiian wear, some of them even to the point of cos-
tumes. He studied the walls around him and considered
options, then snatched a grass skirt, straw hat and several leis. In a flash he went from the guy-on-the-street
to the whacko-at-the-party, but the leis and hat covered
most of his face and the skirt confused the issue. He
walked outside and grabbed a cocktail glass someone
had abandoned on a table. The trick would be to stay
off the bodyguard's radar.

The safest place to get the lay of the land was near
Miguel so he walked that way. "Need some help?" he
asked when he reached the grill.

Miguel looked up from turning chicken kebabs.
"No thanks," he said, then a flicker of recognition lit

his eyes. That was quickly followed by a disbelieving glance at Adam's clothes.

"I'm incognito," Adam said softly.

Miguel smiled, his teeth very white against his brown face. "You look like a cheesy ad for a tiki bar. I wouldn't have known who you were if I hadn't heard your voice. What are you doing here, of all places? You have to know there's more than one gun on this patio that would shoot you dead in an instant. You should go."

"I can't. I'm snooping on Tom Nolan."

"At least tell me you're armed."

"Yeah, I'm armed."

"Brilliant."

"What do you know about Tom Nolan and Aimee?"

"They're tight. I call Nolan 'Little Devin,'" Miguel said.

"Why do you call him that?"

"Well, he took over Holton's wife and his business."

"What about his own wife?"

"She left him a couple of months ago." He handed Adam a pair of tongs. "Make yourself busy. Take the skewers off the grill and put them on that platter." He raised his voice and called his wife, who showed up seconds later. Adam handed Sofia the tray and she winked at him.

After she'd left to distribute the chicken, Adam lowered his voice. "What do you mean he took over Holton's business?"

"Not the human-trafficking thing, that's too much for a lightweight like Nolan. I'm talking about the drug smuggling Holton ran on the side. Small-time, perhaps, but lucrative. Word is Nolan has rubbed a few people the wrong way, though. Ms. Holton better watch it or she'll get caught in the crossfire."

"That explains the bodyguard." Did it also explain the violence against Adam? Why would Tom Nolan care what happened to Adam Parish? As long as he stayed away, so what?

Unless Holton was paying Nolan, but was Nolan connected enough to come up with all these hit people?

Miguel looked around, then lowered his head and spoke. "Don't just stand there thinking like that. There's an icebox by your feet. Hand me something."

Adam did as asked, lifting from the chilled box a tray covered with raw seafood. He glanced over at Nolan as he handed the tray to Miguel. The bodyguard was scanning the crowd and Adam looked away before they made eye contact.

"How about Ms. Holton? Does she know Nolan took over for her husband?"

"Probably. Maybe they're in it together."

Well, he knew she needed money and that her father had turned into a dry well. Maybe she was a partner in this.

"I heard about your marriage," Adam said. "Congratulations."

"Thanks. Ms. Holton said she'd pay us our back wages next week along with a bonus. Once she pays up, I'm taking Sofia away from here. I'm sick of sleeping apart from my bride and I don't want her up here when things go sour."

"I don't blame you," Adam said. He felt the same

way about Chelsea. That's what love was—the desire to protect at any cost.

But, as he was learning, love was also sharing good and bad, danger and peace, everything. In a way, love was allowing yourself to let go of the illusion of control.

What if he'd approached Miguel two days ago? Instead of slinking around learning next to nothing, he could have gotten all this information on Tom Nolan and made inroads into understanding what Aimee was up to. Lesson learned.

He was about to risk moving closer to Aimee and Tom when his phone vibrated in his pocket. "Keep an eye on those two," he said. "Watch for some kind of drug exchange or money or…I don't know, something."

Miguel laughed. Adam picked up a couple of dirty trays and made his way toward the gate that led to the kitchen. Outside the gate, he put the trays down on the table placed there for that purpose and dug his phone out of his pocket.

"Hello?"

"Hey, hombre, this is Diego. I didn't see you today."

"I was on an errand," Adam said. "Listen, can I call you later? I'm in the middle of something—"

"No bother. I just wanted you to know that I heard from every one of those kids and their parents this evening. It was like a parade at my house. Two written apologies and one kid is going to weed the yard every week this summer. Who says there aren't still some responsible parents out there? I'm grateful for what you did. And ultimately, those kids will be grateful, too."

"Thanks," Adam said. "Sounds like you had quite

the day what with the refrigerator thing up here and all that down there."

"Yeah. Wait. What refrigerator thing?"

"Aimee Holton's refrigerator."

"What refrigerator?"

"I heard you discovered the special-order fridge that was delivered last night is the wrong model."

"A refrigerator was delivered last night?" Diego said. "Why wasn't I informed? And it's the wrong one? Wait, we only ordered it a few days ago and it was on back order…it can't be here already."

"I'll ask around and let you know," Adam said. "There's a party here tonight, maybe I misunderstood in all the confusion."

"Man, it's always something with that woman. Okay, I'll check in the morning."

Adam knew he hadn't misunderstood anything. The refrigerator had to be some kind of diversion for a drug drop or something. He needed to talk to Chelsea. He entered the kitchen, where he found both Maria and Sofia fussing with food. "Where's Daisy?" he asked.

"She left with Mariana," Maria said.

"Mariana? The kid with the bruise? What's she doing here at this time of night?"

"I don't know. She was all dressed up but really upset. She and Daisy talked a minute, then Daisy went off with her."

"How long ago?"

"Fifteen minutes or so."

"Where did they go?"

"No idea. She told us to tell you she went to see the goats, whatever that means."

The old goat barn was next door to the shed, where the phony refrigerator had supposedly been delivered. He threw aside his costume and took off through the house, exiting out the front door. The slight breeze whispered an omen through the dead grass as he veered off on the path to the left.

Had someone forced or coerced Mariana into laying a trap for Chelsea?

Had Devin Holton finally organized his next attack?

Chapter Sixteen

Chelsea pulled on Mariana's bloody hand to halt their dash down the hill. In the distance, thanks to the moonlight, she could see what appeared to be the outdoor light for a large new building and the darker shapes beyond it. That must be the old goat farm. The girl stopped abruptly and the two of them almost collided.

"Mariana, tell me what's wrong," Chelsea urged.

The dark shadow of Mariana's head turned to look toward the buildings. "Shhh," she whispered as she turned back. "He'll hear."

"Who'll hear?"

"The guard."

A guard? On a refrigerator?

"What's going on? Where did you get that dress?"

"That man bought it," she said. The girl was attired in the pink dress Chelsea had tried on. The saleswoman's comments played themselves out in Chelsea's mind. "Who is 'that man'?" she demanded.

"It doesn't matter," Mariana said, "Please—"

"First tell me where you went after you broke the

glasses and where we're going now and why," Chelsea insisted.

"I was sent to the barn in the valley," she said so quickly and through so many tears that Chelsea had to concentrate on each uttered word. "Then the fire came and burned some of it and I was brought up here. Last night a truck delivered a whole bunch more girls. Lucia, she's one of them, she was pregnant. One of the men hit her and hit her. Now she's moaning and bleeding— I think she's dying. Please help her."

"How do we get past the guard?" Chelsea asked.

"The way I got out," Mariana said, and took off. Chelsea followed. Once near the building, Mariana slowed way down and the two of them crept past the well-lit front door of the shed and the man sitting on a chair outside of it. They continued their careful trek around the side of the structure until they turned a corner. They were now standing outside the back of the building.

It was very dark. Mariana reached above her head, apparently searching for something on the side of the building. Chelsea suddenly recalled the phone Adam had given her and dug it from her jeans pocket. She turned it on. The light from the screen was enough to reveal that Mariana was attempting to grab a windowsill eight or nine feet off the ground. Chelsea leaned over and cupped her hands, her phone clutched in her teeth. She hefted Mariana up farther against the wall until she could pull herself into the window, where she scuttled about a few seconds, then disappeared inside. That left Chelsea stranded on the ground.

A noise to her left sent her heartbeat racing. She used her phone with the intent to blind whoever was approaching, but the light wasn't bright enough. She directed it to her feet. Shards of broken glass littered the rocky earth and she quickly used the hem of her apron to pick one up to defend herself.

"It's me," a man whispered as he came to a stop a foot or two away. She dropped the shard as his hands grasped her arms. "Chelsea, are you all right?"

"Oh, Adam," she said. "Thank goodness you're here." She pointed up to the window and stuffed the phone in her pocket. "I need a lift up."

"It might be a trap," Adam said. "I'll go first."

"No, you'll terrify Mariana. It's not a trap. Someone is in trouble. Just help me."

He cupped her face and kissed her lips, then pressed his gun into her hands.

"Adam—"

"Please," he said.

She tucked the gun in her waistband as he leaned over. She stepped into his folded hands. As he pushed, she caught the windowsill, cutting her palms on the broken glass caught in the frame. No wonder Mariana's hands had been slippery with blood. She paused in the shallow window, looking down at the dimly lit room below, preparing herself for the jump to the cement floor almost eight feet below. Her body and the baby it nurtured had already been through so much— could she withstand this punishment, too?

Then she finally saw the teetering stack of boxes and old appliances piled up against the wall to her right.

Turning to look down at Adam, she gave him a thumbs-up. The very fact he was here, close by, gave her courage she didn't know she possessed. She turned back to the interior. Mariana appeared below, motioning with one hand for Chelsea to hurry down. Chelsea tore off her apron and laid it over the sill to protect Adam's hands when he followed, then found the top step with the toe of her shoe and climbed down to the floor.

BECAUSE HE HAD approached the building from the bluff side, Adam now took the time to reconnoiter the building's perimeter to find out exactly how well it was guarded. He was relieved when he ascertained there was only one man and he appeared half-asleep.

Then he attacked the window. His first jump fell short. In the near dark, he backed up and then ran forward, jumping at the last minute, catching a cloth of some kind and slipping back to earth with it grasped in his hand. He shook out what he now realized was Chelsea's apron.

Ever aware of the guard, he stuffed part of the apron in his back pocket so as not to leave a red flag behind. He backed up again. This time he caught the sill with one hand, grabbed with the other and, using his feet, managed to attain the opening. Scrunched in the window frame, he peered into the room. There had to be twenty or so teenage girls standing in a semicircle and, as a unit, they turned and stared up at him.

He spied Chelsea on her knees in the middle of the group and scrambled down the makeshift ladder into the hot, humid gloom. The girls parted for him to pass.

He'd never seen so many terrified faces in one place in his life. Chelsea was attending to a young girl lying prone on her back, dried tears on her battered, swollen cheeks, her clothes bloody.

"What's wrong with her?" he asked as he kneeled down.

Chelsea cast him a swift glance. "Her name is Lucia. As far as I can tell, Davy knocked her around this morning. I think she's miscarrying her baby or maybe he ruptured something inside her."

"He did that here?"

"Yes. She was part of the 'shipment' that came in last night in that phony refrigerator delivery. They're waiting now for someone to come load them up and take them to Denver."

He stared at her, too angry for a moment to make a sound.

"Aimee knows what's going on," Chelsea added. "She's been lying about it all day."

"That's why she's so jumpy. She's waiting for the truck to take these kids away."

"That witch," Chelsea muttered. "Lucia's been bleeding for a long time. Her skin is hot and dry. She needs a doctor, Adam. But right now, I need some water to cool her down and something absorbent for the blood."

A young girl wearing a very fancy pink dress and with a bruise on her cheek stepped forward. "I'll take care of it," she said.

"This is Mariana," Chelsea said, smiling at the girl. "Mariana, this is Adam."

"Nice to meet you," Adam said. He turned back to

Chelsea and handed her the red apron. "Have you called the police?"

"I tried but the battery is gone thanks to the fact I used it as a flashlight for too long."

"I'll call." As he pressed the numbers, he asked another question. "Why didn't the other girls escape out the window after Mariana left?"

Chelsea shook her head. "I don't know. I think they're too frightened to move or speak. Most of them are spaced out on drugs. Maybe they didn't want to leave Lucia. Or maybe they don't know where else to go."

The call went through. Adam explained what was going on and added they needed an ambulance as well as police.

"How did Mariana get in the middle of this?" he asked. "You met her before these other kids got here."

"She was a runaway, 'found' by an older man with white hair. Tom Nolan, maybe? I'm not sure. She fought him when he forced her to put on that dress and tried to sell her to his friends. He pawned her off on Aimee, who decided to use her as kitchen help until it was time to ship her off with the others. When Mariana broke the dishes, Aimee dumped her in a barn down in the valley, which I gather is their usual place to stage these transactions, but the fire damaged that place so Mariana was brought up here to wait for the other girls to arrive."

"But how did Mariana get back in that dress? She wasn't wearing it when you saw her the first time, was she?"

"No. I noticed her clothes were too big. Aimee had

given them to her when she got to the house, but once everything went wrong, she made Mariana put the dress back on. That woman is a bitch with a capital *B*."

"She's more than that. All this means she took over Holton's human-trafficking deal," Adam said.

"Along with her 'business associate,' Davy."

"He must be a designated 'recruiter,'" Adam said.

"What's a recruiter?"

"The guy who finds lost, hapless girls, befriends them, gets them dependent on him for drugs, turns them into prostitutes and then sells them. There are too many here for one guy, though. They must have gathered kids from the whole state. There's an underground network in this country to move children sold into sex slavery. Denver is one of the hubs."

Mariana showed up with two bottles of water, a roll of paper towels and a few old rags and items of clothing that Adam passed along to Chelsea.

He had a decision to make. Should he get Mariana to help him move the girls' outside via the broken window and into the old goat barn so they weren't trapped in this building? Or did he go outside and take care of the situation from there until the police showed up? They were still almost thirty minutes away...

Once again, he scanned the faces around him and decided on the latter. The girls were frightened, impaired and cowed by abuse. He wasn't even sure the goat barn would hold all of them or what shelter it would provide.

"It's going on midnight," he told Chelsea. "I don't think we have much time before that truck gets here.

I hate to leave you alone with Lucia, but I need to go subdue the guard."

"Take the gun," she said as she reached for it.

"No," he said, catching her hands. "You keep it. Anyone comes through that door, use it."

"But Adam—"

"I can't leave you and the kids here unprotected. I'll 'borrow' the guard's gun, don't worry. Caution the kids to stay away from the door and try to stay out of sight. I love you, Chelsea."

She looked up at him as he stood. "I love you, too," she said.

ADAM RAN UP the dark hill, then circled back and approached the building from the road. He walked toward the pool of light by the main door, where the guard sat in a chair. The man stood as he caught sight of Adam.

"Who are you?" he asked.

Adam kept advancing. He fiddled with his pocket as though to show identification at the same time he spoke. "Davy said the truck will be here any second."

"I know. I just got word they're five minutes out."

Adam stopped a foot or so in front of the man, made as if to show him identity and instead delivered a very fast blow to the man's jaw. He went down in a flash. Adam dragged him to the side of the barn and quickly relieved him of his weapon. He checked it to make sure it was loaded. He also took his keys, flashlight, hat and jacket. He used the guard's handcuffs to attach him to a drainage pipe and gagged him with his own necktie.

Satisfied, Adam shrugged on the jacket. It was tight but manageable. Now to unlock the shed. The noise of an engine and the creak of old springs alerted him that a vehicle was approaching, sans headlights. He saw its dark shape stop, turn and back toward the shed door.

Adam walked quickly back to the guard's post, arriving in the pool of outdoor light right as the driver jumped out of the truck, a shotgun gripped in his hand. The passenger was half his size. He darted to the back of the truck, where he rolled open the back gate.

"Who the hell are you?" the driver asked as Adam approached.

"The other guy got sick. Davy sent me down here to relieve him," Adam said as he glanced into the now open back of the truck. Lines of wooden benches ran along either side. No windows, nothing to hold on to. His stomach turned as he thought of those poor scared kids riding in the sinister enclave of this joyless truck.

"Open the shed," the driver said. "We haven't got all night.

"It's hot out here, Lou," the passenger complained as he mopped his forehead with his sleeve. "I haven't eaten anything since noon. I don't know why—"

"Stop complaining," Lou said. "Cripes, Bennie, you drive me nuts." He pointed the shotgun at Adam as if to motivate him. "Open the shed."

These were the same two guys from the night before, Adam was sure of it. He found the right key. "One of the girls isn't well," he said as he swung open the door. "She needs a doctor."

"That's Denver's problem."

"She might be dead by Denver."

Lou shrugged. "Hurry it up. We've got a long way to go tonight."

Lou and Bennie both strolled into the dimly lit shed with authority, shining powerful flashlights, highlighting a bevy of frightened faces, including Mariana's but not Chelsea's. Adam's gaze went immediately to the open window in the back—he half expected to find her hiding up there. Nothing. Mariana met his gaze and looked away.

The driver strode right over to Lucia, then called over his shoulder, "Bennie, get the girls into the truck."

Bennie started yelling in very bad Spanish interspersed with equally poor English. The girls began moving outside. Adam glanced at Lou to find that he'd kneeled down to study Lucia's condition more closely. As soon as Bennie looked away to reprimand one of the kids, Adam drew his stolen gun and slammed the grip hard against the guy's round head, catching him as he slumped to the floor. He pocketed the man's gun, worried for a moment the commotion would catch Lou's attention, but the guy remained on his knees.

Adam crept forward until he was close enough to shove the barrel against the base of Lou's skull. "Drop your weapon," he said.

Lou didn't move.

"A shot will paralyze you if it doesn't kill you first," Adam added. "Now, put the shotgun on the floor and push it away."

The weapon clattered against the cement floor. The man shoved it off with his right hand.

"Stand up."

"Who *are* you?" Lou snarled as he heaved himself upright.

"No friend of yours," Adam said. He carefully retrieved the shotgun, then dragged a dazed-looking Bennie to his feet and prodded both men toward the door. The girls parted to let them pass.

They had just cleared the shed when another man approached from around the truck, his arm around Chelsea's neck, a revolver pushed against her temple. Davy had finally made an appearance.

"Stop right there," he called.

Adam looked right into Chelsea's eyes. "Don't do anything he says," she said and paid for the remark as Davy tightened the arm around her neck.

"Stay where you are or I shoot her," he growled. "Lou, take the shotgun and frisk him." Lou paused. "It's okay," Davy prompted. "He's not going to fire at you because he knows if he does I'll kill this pretty little cook and then I'll kill him and then I'll still do anything I want with the girls."

"You won't risk a house full of Aimee's guests hearing gunshots," Adam said.

"Are you kidding? Why do you think the music is so loud?"

"The police are coming," Chelsea added, her voice hoarse.

"Let 'em come. Go on, Lou. Do what I told you."

Lou took all three weapons from Adam, then smashed

his fist into Adam's jaw. He would have kept it up if Davy hadn't yelled at him to stop.

"Get the girls into the truck," Davy ordered, "and then get the hell out of here."

Bennie kind of staggered away but Lou took out his aggression by shoving the nearest teens past Adam. Mariana was one of them. As she passed Adam she whispered, *"Mira en el delantal."*

He frowned as he tried to make sense of what she said but his thoughts quickly moved on as Davy pushed Chelsea toward him. He caught her before she fell. "You two, back inside."

The trunk gate clanked closed behind the last girl and Lou secured it with a big padlock. Adam wrapped his arm around Chelsea's waist and did as directed. It felt like a death march.

"I'm sorry," she whispered as they walked. "I thought I could help if I was outside but Davy found me hiding over by the guard you must have knocked out."

"Don't worry, it's okay," he told her and kissed her hair.

"By the way," she added, "I think we should get married right this moment. Here and now. Forever. I love you, Adam."

He kissed her again.

"Okay lovebirds, that's far enough," Davy said, but his attention was immediately diverted as he caught sight of Lucia tossing and turning on the bed of castoffs Chelsea and Mariana had created for her. Something red draped her body.

"Who the hell is that?" he demanded.

"She's the girl you all but killed today," Chelsea said.

"Oh, the knocked-up one. She's not your main problem right now."

Adam realized the red cloth was Chelsea's apron. Mariana had whispered something about an apron—what other one but this? She'd said to look at it but all he saw was an apron.

"You two have really screwed this up for me," Davy said. "What am I going to do with your dead bodies?"

"Here's an idea," Adam said, his mind working on how to examine that apron. "Don't kill us."

"It's too late for that." Davy studied Chelsea. "Such a shame because you, babe, are a beaut. All that red hair. I bet you're hot, aren't you?"

"Hot enough to burn you to a cinder," Chelsea said defiantly. He grabbed her and roughly kissed her. Adam rushed him, but Davy once again used Chelsea as a shield and fired a bullet. It grazed Adam's left arm. Chelsea screamed. Davy slapped her with the gun so hard she fell to the floor. Adam heard her head hit the cement and in a flash, he kneeled beside her. That put him close to the red apron. It was turned so the pocket was hidden next to Lucia.

Davy paced nearby, the gun trained on them, but his brow furrowed. It looked like he wasn't used to doing his own dirty work, as though intimidating little girls was more his style. Chelsea moaned and Davy stopped pacing, his gaze riveted to her pale face, the gun clutched in a white-knuckled fist. It was like he longed to squish a bug but was too squeamish. Adam knew Davy would get over that as he considered his options.

He used the man's distraction to drag the apron from Lucia and was immediately aware of the heavy shape inside the long pocket. When the garment bumped against his thigh, he knew. The object in the pocket was a gun and odds were good it was the one he'd left with Chelsea. She must have given it to Mariana when she left the shed and Mariana had then hidden it in the apron. He slid his hand in the pocket. His fingers closed around the grip. Without a second's hesitation, he raised the weapon. Davy, sensing movement, turned. Adam fired—the bullet hit Davy right between the eyes and he went down like a ton of broken bricks.

Ignoring the fallen man, Adam rushed to gather Chelsea in his arms right as headlights shone into the shed. Thank goodness, help had arrived! As he gently lay her head back down, it finally registered on him there were no flashing lights, no sirens.

What now, or better yet, who now? He moved cautiously to the front of the shed, gun drawn.

A familiar shape emerged from a police vehicle with a darkened rack on top of the car.

"Whip?" Adam said.

"Good God almighty!" Whip said, his gun drawn. "Adam? Lord, boy, have you been shot?"

"It's nothing," Adam said for the first time recognizing the searing pain in his left upper arm. "I'm just so glad to see you. Get on the radio, get ambulances. There's a van full of kidnapped minors on their way to Denver." He stepped closer and handed Whip his gun. "This is the weapon used to kill the guy inside. It belongs to the guard, but I did the shooting." His voice petered out as he noticed Whip didn't lower his weapon.

"Whip?"

"Where's Chelsea?" he asked.

"She's unconscious back in the shed. We need an ambulance—"

"Is this where you've been holed up? Man, I'd laugh if I didn't want to cry. Why didn't you leave?"

"We had something to finish—"

"Finish? Is that what you call this?" Whip swore under his breath. "I begged you not to come to Arizona but I always knew you would."

"I had to find out who was trying to kill me and why," Adam said, stepping back. What was going on?

"When your friend Dennis told me about finding that box I knew eventually you'd come for it. I tried to steal it but he'd locked it away by then. Then you said something yesterday about a friend and I knew it was Dennis, I knew."

"Whip, what's in that box?" Adam said, an ominous feeling growing in his gut.

"I wanted you stopped but not here, not by me," Whip continued.

"Listen," Adam said, "first things first. We need to get help for Chelsea and the girl—"

"What girl?"

"The man I just killed, his name is Davy, he beat up a fourteen-year-old. She's burning up and—"

"Is she wearing a pink dress?"

"No, she's one of the new kids—wait. How do you know Mariana?" Adam asked as shivers ran up his spine. Was it possible Mariana's tormentor wasn't Tom Nolan, but…

"Damn Davy," Whip grumbled. "Thinks he knows everything. I've been in this business for more than a decade, taking partners when I had to. Holton was a screwup, but I swear, Aimee is worse. When she brought in Davy things went from manageable to chaos."

Adam stared at Whip. His head told him things his heart didn't want to hear and for several seconds, the ensuing battle of truth vs. wishful thinking deafened him. Whip's mouth moved but Adam couldn't decipher a single word until all of a sudden, sound returned like a sonic boom. "I had everything under control," Whip said.

"You're in on this," Adam said woodenly. "My God, you're not only in on it, you started it. You and Ballard—"

"Ballard?" Whip scoffed. "No, I found someone else in the system who needed cash. When Ballard found out this guy sold you out, he came looking for me."

"He drew the gun because he saw you coming up behind me," Adam said.

"Yep, but he wasn't fast enough. Now he's under five feet of desert sand. It pains me, it truly does, that you and your girl will soon be lying right alongside him."

Adam stared at a man he once thought he knew inside and out. "Has everything about you been a lie?"

"Just about," Whip admitted.

"For how long?"

"Forever."

"You were searching for the box after my father died.

That's why you wanted to renovate the house, so you could look for it. What in the world is inside it?"

He shook his head. "I'm not sure," he said finally. "Okay, go back inside. I'll make it quick."

"The police, ambulances—"

"All canceled. No one's going to ride to your rescue. Go hold Chelsea's hand. Tell her you love her. It's your last chance."

Adam stood his ground. His head throbbed with disbelief and yet discrepancies in Whip's behavior began to eat through his denial. Ballard's shooting, sure, but even before that.

"I'll shoot you right here if I have to," Whip said.

"No, you won't," Chelsea said from behind Adam.

Adam turned and there she was, framed in the doorway, Davy's gun clutched in her hands. She might be deathly pale but she was also strong and beautiful and when she smiled at him, her whole face looked…different.

"Give the gun to Adam, Whip. I used Davy's phone, the police are on their way."

Whip made no effort to do as she said.

"You're the man Mariana told me about," Chelsea continued. "You're a depraved and evil soul. No more killing. It's over. Give Adam your gun."

The silence was deafening.

"Move out of the way, Adam," she said.

The truth was he couldn't move. His feet just wouldn't budge.

The silence stretched on until Whip shook his head.

"She's right," he said, his voice incredulous, his gun hand sinking to his side. "It is over."

Adam reached for the weapon.

Whip met his gaze. "It's over," he repeated and in a flash, he'd pointed the gun at his own temple. "Over."

Adam closed his eyes as Whip pulled the trigger.

Epilogue

One week later

"I'm ready to open it," Adam said and, taking a knife, slit through the tape.

Chelsea had wondered when he would be able to face the box. Unwilling for anyone to see what was inside it until he did, Adam had taken the cardboard container from Whip's car and hidden it in their van before the cops got there, before Lucia had been whisked to safety by an ambulance or Aimee Holton had been led away in handcuffs or Tom Nolan had been caught red-handed in a high-stakes drug deal with who else but the television actor.

Truth be told, the last few days had been wonderful. Without a vendetta against them, they'd had time to enjoy each other, enhanced by the miraculous fact Chelsea's memory was back. She credited Davy's push and the subsequent bash of her head against the cement. Adam was prone to saying his guardian angel had woken her just in time. Whatever, the fact was she now had a past. Her mom and dad, her sisters, her brother Bill, her grandmother's face, her cute little food truck, her cat, her apartment, her overdue book—she had all that. And thanks to the baby growing in her body and the man sitting six inches to her right, she had a future.

All the pain and anger she'd assumed would engulf her once her memory returned had not happened. She'd already worked through all those feelings because while Steven had morphed into Adam, she had morphed, as well. She knew what it was like to be almost two different people, but not quite, not really.

And Chelsea's next goal was to help Mariana discover the same thing about herself. The police had stopped the truck before it crossed the state line and the girls had been delivered into child protective services. Mariana couldn't go home to her abusive parents so Chelsea had arranged to take her in. That meant relocating to Arizona, but Adam and his pal Dennis had big plans to build a tavern and she was open to anything as long as they were together. The important thing was that Mariana understood she had survived largely due to her own wits, that she was strong and unique and the future need not be a reflection of the past. Adam was as anxious to help Mariana as she was, so it looked as though before she gave birth to their own child, they would have Mariana to parent.

Adam, whose injured arm had healed as fast as all his other wounds seemed to, spread open the box flaps and removed a piece of dusty plastic revealing a diary with his mother's name written on the cover. Tucked inside were a couple of pieces of paper clipped together.

"This is Dad's writing," he said as he looked at the papers. "I'm starting with them."

She sat back as he read to himself, content to be here if he needed her, anticipating what he would really need was time to assimilate what he learned.

She'd almost dozed off when he put down the papers and looked at her. "I guess I should be flabbergasted, but after everything that's happened...at least now I know the truth."

She waited as he gathered his thoughts.

His voice was soft when he finally spoke. "I'll paraphrase what I've learned, okay? Unbeknownst to me, it seems my mother suspected that Whip was the guy who seduced her student into running away. He was a young cop then, as fit and strong as his nickname implied. When she confronted him he told her she was mistaken. She talked to Dad but he didn't believe her. He argued that poking around would only jeopardize their friendship. In other words, he stood by Whip instead of her. And apparently, he told Whip that Mom kept a diary."

Chelsea didn't say a word. What could she say?

"So, my mom made an appointment to talk to the chief," Adam continued. "You know, to elicit his help. Whip got wind of this and decided to steal her diary while she was at the appointment, but she was running late and surprised him by being home. Panicked, he killed her and searched for the diary, but couldn't find where she'd hidden it. Dad learned all this later."

"Good grief. Whip killed your mother."

Adam nodded. "Yeah, and then hinted to me that Dad had done it."

"Oh, Adam."

"Dad felt guilty about not supporting Mom, by letting her down before her death…about everything. Then he found her diary and read it. Apparently, after she talked to Whip about her student, he started showing up the same places she was. She felt threatened. If she told Dad this part, he was too drunk to remember it and that just fed his guilt. He talked to Whip, hoping he was wrong, but Whip admitted everything I told you before. He said the chief would never believe a drunk, not when Whip had a different story. That's when my father put all their old love letters and the diary and these two little pieces of paper into a box and hid it under the house. I don't think I'll ever know if he killed himself or just died from guilt."

"Maybe it doesn't matter," Chelsea said gently.

"He could have shown the chief the diary. He could have fought Whip and ultimately saved who knows how many other kids. But he didn't. He was a coward."

"But you're not," Chelsea said. "And maybe now you can find some peace with the past. You're going to need it with Mariana and your own child to raise."

"I know." He stared at the box and then looked down at her, melting her with his gray gaze. "I'll look at the rest later, then I'll figure out what to do with it."

She nestled against him. "That sounds like a good idea."

"I have an even better idea," he told her as he tipped her chin and claimed her lips.

* * * * *

*Look for more books from Alice Sharpe
later in 2019!*

I N T R I G U E

Available March 19, 2019

#1845 MARINE FORCE RECON
Declan's Defenders • by Elle James

Former marine Declan O'Neill set up a vigilante task force, and his first mission involves helping Grace Lawrence find her missing roommate. Will they be able to locate the woman before her unearthed secrets endanger them all?

#1846 HER ALIBI
by Carol Ericson

Although he was once a cop, Connor Wells agrees to help Savannah Martell, the woman he has always loved, after she tells him she is being framed for her ex-husband's murder—but is he protecting a killer?

#1847 ICE COLD KILLER
Eagle Mountain Murder Mystery: Winter Storm Wedding
by Cindi Myers

A winter storm is blocking the only road in and out of Eagle Mountain, Colorado, and a serial killer is on the loose. To protect the town, State Patrol officer Ryder Stewart and grieving veterinarian Darcy Marsh will need to work together to fight an unknown assailant—and their attraction to each other.

#1848 SMOKY MOUNTAINS RANGER
The Mighty McKenzies • by Lena Diaz

When ranger Adam McKenzie sees a woman being threatened, he vows to do whatever it takes to protect her. But private investigator Jody Ingram knows nothing about the gunmen she is running from. Can Adam save Jody from the unknown forces that threaten her?

#1849 WYOMING COWBOY MARINE
Carsons & Delaneys: Battle Tested • by Nicole Helm

After Hilly Adams reports a missing person who doesn't seem to exist, Cam Delaney takes it upon himself to investigate the situation. Suddenly, people are after Hilly, and Cam must step in to protect the strange woman. Who is she... and who is the man who disappeared?

#1850 UNDERCOVER JUSTICE
by Nico Rosso

Stephanie Shun and Arash Shamshiri infiltrated a dangerous gang...but they each don't know the other is undercover. Will the truth about their identities bring them together or tear them apart?

Get 4 FREE REWARDS!

We'll send you 2 FREE Books
plus 2 FREE Mystery Gifts.

Harlequin Intrigue® books feature heroes and heroines that confront and survive danger while finding themselves irresistibly drawn to one another.

FREE Value Over **$20**

YES! Please send me 2 FREE Harlequin Intrigue® novels and my 2 FREE gifts (gifts are worth about $10 retail). After receiving them, if I don't wish to receive any more books, I can return the shipping statement marked "cancel." If I don't cancel, I will receive 6 brand-new novels every month and be billed just $4.99 each for the regular-print edition or $5.74 each for the larger-print edition in the U.S., or $5.74 each for the regular-print edition or $6.49 each for the larger-print edition in Canada. That's a savings of at least 12% off the cover price! It's quite a bargain! Shipping and handling is just 50¢ per book in the U.S. and 75¢ per book in Canada.* I understand that accepting the 2 free books and gifts places me under no obligation to buy anything. I can always return a shipment and cancel at any time. The free books and gifts are mine to keep no matter what I decide.

Choose one: ☐ **Harlequin Intrigue®**
Regular-Print
(182/382 HDN GMYW)

☐ **Harlequin Intrigue®**
Larger-Print
(199/399 HDN GMYW)

Name (please print)

Address   Apt. #

City   State/Province   Zip/Postal Code

Mail to the **Reader Service:**
IN U.S.A.: P.O. Box 1341, Buffalo, NY 14240-8531
IN CANADA: P.O. Box 603, Fort Erie, Ontario L2A 5X3

Want to try 2 free books from another series! Call 1-800-873-8635 or visit www.ReaderService.com.

Declan O'Neill hiked his rucksack higher on his shoulders
and trudged down the sidewalk in downtown Washington,
DC. The last time he'd seen so many people in one place,
he'd been a fresh recruit at US Marine Corps basic training
in San Diego, California, standing among a bunch of
teenagers, just like him, being processed into the military.

He shouldered his way through the throngs of
sightseers, businessmen and career women hurrying to the
next building along the road. The sun shone on a bright
spring day. Cherry blossoms exploded in fluffy pinkish-
white, dripping petals onto the lawns and sidewalks in an
optimistic display of hope.

Hope.

Declan snorted. Here he was, eleven years after joining
the US Marine Corps...eleven years of knowing what was
expected of him, of not having to decide what to wear each
day. Eleven years of a steady paycheck, no matter how

small, in an honorable profession, making a difference in the world.

Now he was faced with the daunting task of job hunting with a huge strike on his record.

But not today.

Why he'd decided to take the train from Bethesda, Maryland, to the political hub of the entire country was beyond his own comprehension. But with nowhere else to go and nothing holding him back—no job, no family, no home—he'd thought, "Why not?"

He'd never been to the White House, never stopped to admire the Declaration of Independence, drafted by the forefathers of his country and he'd never stood at the foot of the Lincoln Memorial, in the shadow of the likeness of Abraham Lincoln, a leader who'd set the United States on a revolutionary course. He'd never been to the Vietnam War Memorial or any other memorial in DC.

Yeah. And so what?

Sightseeing wouldn't pay the bills. Out of the military, out of money and sporting a dishonorable discharge, Declan would be hard-pressed to find a decent job. Who would hire a man whose only skills were superb marksmanship that allowed him to kill a man from four hundred yards away, expertise in hand-to-hand combat and the ability to navigate himself out of a paper bag with nothing more than the stars and his wits?

Don't miss
Marine Force Recon *by Elle James,*
available April 2019 wherever
Harlequin® *Intrigue books and ebooks are sold.*

www.Harlequin.com

SPECIAL EXCERPT FROM

H

HQN™

A blizzard is keeping guests at Sterling Montana Guest Ranch, where a killer is lurking in the shadows.

Read on for a sneak preview of
Stroke of Luck *by New York Times and USA TODAY bestselling author B.J. Daniels.*

"Bad luck always comes in threes."

Standing in the large kitchen of the Sterling Montana Guest Ranch, Will Sterling shot the woman an impatient look. "I don't have time for this right now, Dorothea."

"Just sayin'," Dorothea Brand muttered under her breath. The fifty-year-old housekeeper was short and stout with a helmet of dark hair and piercing dark eyes. She'd been a fixture on the ranch since Will and his brothers were kids, which made her invaluable, but also as bossy as an old mother hen.

After the Sterling boys had lost their mother, Dorothea had stepped in. Their father, Wyatt, had continued to run the guest ranch alone and then with the help of his sons until his death last year. For the first time, Will would finally be running the guest ranch without his father calling all the shots. He'd been looking forward to the challenge and to carrying on the family business.

But now his cook was laid up with a broken leg? He definitely didn't like the way the season was starting, Will thought as the housekeeper leaned against the counter, giving him one of her you're-going-to-regret-this looks as he considered who he could call.

As his brother Garrett brought in a box of supplies from town, Will asked, "Do you know anyone who can cook?"

"What about Poppy Carmichael?" Garrett suggested as he pulled a bottle of water from the refrigerator, opened it and took a long drink. "She's a caterer now."

Will frowned. "Poppy?" An image appeared of a girl with freckles, braces, skinned knees and reddish-brown hair in pigtails. "I haven't thought of Poppy in years. I thought she moved away."

"She did, but she came back about six months ago and started a catering business in Whitefish," Garrett said. "I only know because I ran into her at a party recently. The food was really good, if that helps."

"Wait, I remember her. Cute kid. Didn't her father work for the forest service?" their younger brother Shade asked as he also came into the kitchen with a box of supplies. He deposited the box inside the large pantry just off the kitchen. "Last box," he announced, dusting off his hands.

"You remember, Will. Poppy and her dad lived in the old forest service cabin a mile or so from here," Garrett said, grinning at him. "She used to ride her bike over here and help us with our chores. At least, that was her excuse."

Will avoided his brother's gaze. It wasn't like he'd ever forgotten.

"I just remember the day she decided to ride Lightning," Shade said. "She climbed up on the corral, and as the horse ran by, she jumped on it!" He shook his head, clearly filled with admiration. "I can't imagine what she thought she was going to do, riding him bareback." He laughed. "She stayed on a lot longer than I thought she would. But it's a wonder she didn't kill herself. The girl had grit. But I always wondered what possessed her to do that."

Garrett laughed and shot another look at Will. "She was trying to impress our brother."

"That poor little girl was smitten," Dorothea agreed as she narrowed her dark gaze at Will. "And you, being fifteen and full of yourself, often didn't give her the time of day. So what could possibly go wrong hiring her to cook for you?"

Don't miss
Stroke of Luck *by B.J. Daniels, available March 2019*
wherever HQN Books and ebooks are sold.

www.Harlequin.com

PHBJDEXP0319